Mary's Evolution

Mary's Erotic Adventures, Volume 2

P.T. Brown

Published by Guinea Pig Publishing, 2023.

MARY'S EVOLUTION

First edition. May 9, 2023.

Copyright © 2023 P.T. Brown.

ISBN: 979-8223337133

Written by P.T. Brown.

Also by P.T. Brown

Mary's Erotic Adventures
Mary's Awakening
Mary's Evolution

Standalone
Sophie's Hotwife Adventures

Chapter 1

It had been a month since Richard left the country. He and Mary had kept in touch, but his work assignment in Germany was looking long-term and their sexting had started to become less and less frequent. Mary didn't mind of course. She was surprised it had lasted as long as it did. She really missed their bedroom antics, but she had been using Elliot to plug the gap Richard had left in her sex life pretty well, and Elliot wasn't complaining either. Her problem was that she was always having to take the lead, so screwing Elliot was quickly becoming as mundane as it was before she'd had her eyes - and her legs - opened by the fling with her now-absent sexy older man.

Her newly established close friendship with Louise was developing well. They had always been reasonably distant friends at university amongst a larger group, but since Louise's chance involvement with the Richard situation, then having sex with his friend Mike, she and Mary had developed a secret bond which meant that they would have many private conversations away from the others. One Thursday afternoon, Mary and Louise were sat together in the sun during a break between lectures.

"Got any plans for tomorrow night?" Louise asked.

"Not really, why?" Mary asked.

"Fancy wine and a film in your room? My housemates are getting fucking annoying. Every Friday and Saturday they seem to want to stay up all night partying. It's getting more than a little repetitive now."

Mary laughed, "you're usually the life and soul of the party."

"I know, but the same shit every single week. It's just too much. And the guys they bring back-"

"You're welcome at mine any time," Mary interrupted. "Why don't you stay over? I know I'm down to a single bed since moving back from Margaret's, but I'm sure there's room for two of us."

"You sure? That would be great."

"It'll cost you a bottle of wine though," Mary said, smiling.

"I'll bring two. And snacks."

"Then you have yourself a date," Mary said, "now we better get back to lectures before we're missed."

That night Mary was sat on her bed watching TV when her phone pinged. It was Richard.

'Hey there. x'

'Hey. x'

'Doing anyone exciting this weekend?'

'No, night in with Louise tomorrow. She's staying over for wine and a film. You?'

'Maybe, hot brunette, but she's got nothing on you! So, you're having sex with Louise tomorrow? x'

Mary hesitated. She'd not given that a thought. During their night of debauchery with Richard and Mike she and Louise did have a little fun together which they both enjoyed, but nothing like that had happened since, but then they hadn't been alone together in bed since either. She smiled to herself.

'Maybe. x'

'Do it. Enjoy it. Speak soon. x'

'x'

Mary sat back on her bed and frowned to herself for a second, then smiled, remembering her last encounter with Louise and the two men. She decided to test the water with Louise.

'Hey, don't bring anything too thick to sleep in. This bed is small, and the room is always warm. #JustSaying.'

A moment later Louise responded.

'I wasn't planning on us sleeping in anything. #Naked #Sex #FWB'

'You read my mind. #excited. Coming straight from lectures?'

'Yep.'

'Yay, better go shave tonight then.'

'Yes, me too. You look great shaved x'

Mary smiled to herself. She was a little nervous at the thought. Her last sexual encounter with Louise wasn't pre-meditated, and she didn't have time to think too much about Louise sliding down her body and putting her tongue inside her. This was different, but she wanted to do it, and Louise was not only very sexy but also very skilled, as far as Mary could remember. She headed off to the bathroom and shaved her legs and her pubic hair entirely before having an early night.

The next day Mary headed to lectures with a spring in her step. Despite the fact she knew she was on a promise, she also knew that Louise responded to Mary's most feminine side so had dressed for the day in a short dress she knew Louise liked, as she had commented on it before, and a little pair of boots. Luckily the Indian summer they were having allowed for it, otherwise she would have looked stupid and been very cold. As she strolled up to their group of friends, Louise looked through the crowd of people to see her and smiled, Mary looked at Louise's outfit smiled back. While Louise had a very similar slight figure to Mary, she was more a tight jeans and knee-high boots girl. Usually anyway. Today she had a dress on not too dissimilar to Mary's, which really floated Mary's boat. Throughout lectures that day they kept exchanging glances, not really bothered if anyone else noticed.

As they left lectures Louise chatted to a few of their friends and grabbed her overnight bag from the back of the room while Mary went outside for a cigarette.

"Hey," Elliot said as he wandered over to her, "you look nice. Hot date?"

Mary was about to respond but didn't get the chance.

"Me," Louise said from behind him as she followed him over to Mary.

"Really?" Elliot asked, looking Mary in the eye.

"Really!" Mary replied as Louise stood next to her and leaned into her a little.

"Fuck. Can I come?" he asked, laughing a little.

"Not a fucking chance. Tonight, she's mine," Louise said.

Elliot's eyes glistened.

"And on that note, shall we go?" Louise asked turning to Mary.

Mary smiled and turned.

"See you Monday," she said over her shoulder as they wandered off together across campus, leaving Elliot stood alone and a little stunned.

When they arrived at Mary's room, she started to feel a little nervous, and Louise detected it straight away.

"Hey, it's just me," she said, taking off her coat and hanging it on the back of the door in the small room.

"I know," Mary said. "It's just..."

"Shhh," Louise said interrupting her, "come here."

Mary stepped over to Louise nervously.

"Close your eyes," Louise said softly. Mary obliged.

Louise leaned in and kissed her, deeply. Mary instantly remembered how much she had enjoyed kissing Louise, and her nerves started to fall away as she kissed Louise back. They stood for ages, arms around each other exploring each other's mouths with their tongues. Louise eventually slowed and stepped back.

"I'd forgotten how much I like kissing you," she said as Mary took off her coat.

"I hadn't," Mary said, smiling over her shoulder at Louise as she hung up her coat. "Shall we go and cook the Pizza? Then we can settle down and not really have to leave the room again other than for the loo."

"Let's," Louise said.

They cooked the pizzas and put Louise's wine in the fridge, taking out one of Mary's stock wines and heading back to her room. They sat on the bed together, legs crossed facing each other eating the pizza and chatting while they quickly polished off their food and the first bottle of wine.

"I best get another bottle, and I need a wee," Mary said, taking the plates and the empty bottle and heading for the door.

"Don't be too long," Louise said, seductively.

Mary blinked at her and headed out of the door. While she was gone, Louise took off her boots and socks, tapping her foot impatiently. A few moments later, Mary returned, armed with a replacement bottle of wine. She put it on the table and put something in her drawer, then sat down on the bed next to Louise.

"Now," Louise said, "where were we?"

Mary, now more confident after half a bottle of wine and their earlier kiss, turned and put her hand on Louise's shoulder, pulling her in for another kiss. As Louise leaned forward, she put her hand on Mary's thigh, sending a pleasurable shiver through her body. They kissed for a while, and eventually Louise took the lead.

"Stand up," she said.

Mary stood and turned to face her. Louise slid forward so she was sat on the edge of the bed with Mary's body in front of her. She lifted the bottom of Mary's dress, and Mary took the bottom of it and lifted it up and over her head, dropping it to the floor. Louise looked up at Mary's naked body, surprised.

"I'm sure you had at least a bra on earlier."

"Oh, I did, and a thong. Took them off in the loo," Mary said, smiling.

Louise smiled back, and leaned forward, kissing Mary's tummy softly for a moment.

"I didn't get that memo."

She leaned forward again, and kissed the top of Mary's leg, achingly close to her sex.

"Have you got the memo now?" Mary asked, becoming more aroused and wetter by the second.

Louise stood up and slid her dress over her head, dropping it on top of Mary's, then quickly unclipped her bra and let it fall to the floor.

Mary, brimming with confidence, knelt and tugged Louise's thong to the floor before standing back up and looking into Louise's eyes.

"You forgot something," Louise said.

"What?" Mary looked puzzled.

"They look great, but you still have your sexy little boots on," Louise said, looking down.

"My bad," Mary giggled.

She sat down on the bed and leaned forward, quickly removing her boots and socks before looking up at the naked Louise, who was smiling down at her.

"Put your lamp on," Louise said, as she wandered over to the door and turned the main light off.

Mary lay on the bed on her front and leaned over the headboard to her lamp, turning it on. Before she could turn back, she felt Louise's hands on her back, then her legs resting either side of her hips as Louise straddled her body and rested her weight on Mary's bottom. Mary murmured her approval.

"So," Louise said, caressing Mary's back.

"So," Mary replied, her eyes glistening in the light.

Louise leaned forward and started to kiss Mary's shoulder blades softly, working down her spine slowly and sliding her body back each time allowing her to continue kissing until she reached the small of Mary's back. Mary was lost in the moment, arching her back and raising her bottom, encouraging Louise to go further. Louise took the hint and kissed Mary's cheeks, then moved back to the centre, drawing a line with her tongue from the base of Mary's spine, slowly lower, stopping just a hair's breadth short of her rear opening. Mary whimpered a little and Louise smiled, pleased with herself for teasing.

"Roll over," Louise instructed.

Mary did as she was told, and Louise slowly leaned forward and pressed her body on top of her. Mary wrapped a leg around Louise's body, and they started to kiss once more. Louise placed a hand on

Mary's shoulder then slowly slid her nails downward, digging in painfully but pleasantly to Mary's soft skin until they reached her nipple. Louise opened her hand and squeezed Mary's breast. Mary moaned through Louise's kisses. Louise smiled, then continued sliding her hand down Mary's body until she reached her clit. She rubbed it gently, just enough for Mary to react to it, before sliding down and slipping her fingers into Mary's soaking wet opening.

"God you're wet," she whispered in Mary's ear, tugging on her g-spot and making her moan.

"It's your fucking fault." Mary replied through gentle moans.

"I need to taste you," Louise whispered.

"Don't let me stop you," Mary moaned.

Louise slid down Mary's body quickly and replaced her fingers with her tongue. Switching between Mary's clit and burying her tongue deep inside her opening, both women moaning with pleasure. After a few minutes, Mary felt selfish.

"Don't you have anything for me to do?" she whispered eagerly between her moans.

"I thought you'd never ask," Louise said happily, "slide down the bed a bit and lie on your side."

Louise stood and Mary slid down a little, allowing room at the top for Louise to lie next to her in a sixty-nine.

"Just remember this is my first time," Mary said timidly.

"I have no doubt you'll pick it up really quickly," Louise said, as both women lay next to each other and lifted their free leg allowing their mouths to access each other fully.

Louise went back to working on Mary immediately, which did a lot for Mary's confidence as she studied Louise's shaven sex right in front of her face. She leaned forward and kissed Louise's clit gently. Louise moaned in approval. She ran her tongue over it. Louise moaned again, arching her pelvis forward to encourage her. Mary tasted Louise on her tongue. She liked it and wanted more. She leaned her head forward and started to mimic what Louise was doing to her, then she felt Louise bury her tongue deep inside her. Mary closed her eyes and did the same.

The warmth and wetness of Louise's sex was overwhelming, and her reaction to Mary pleasuring her was obvious, given her moaning and writhing. Mary was inspired and set about Louise's body with her tongue quite aggressively as she wrapped her legs around Louise's head, encouraging her do the same. After a few minutes Mary released Louise's head from her grasp, and both slowed their oral pleasure on each other. Louise stopped first, standing up and bending over to kiss Mary briefly before reaching for their wine glasses.

Mary lit a cigarette and they both sat naked together as they drank wine and Louise continued stroking the inside of Mary's thigh.

"You taste good," Louise said, smiling to herself.

"So do you," Mary replied, "was I ok? You know?"

"More than ok. If that was your first time, I can't wait to see what your second is like."

Mary smiled, a little embarrassed, but pleased with herself.

"Shall we put that film?" Louise suggested.

"I'm up for that," Mary said.

They finished the contents of their glasses and put on the film. Mary lay on the bed and Louise lay behind her, spooning her and slowly running her fingertips over Mary's body as they enjoyed lying there naked together.

When the film finished, Mary flicked off the TV and rolled over to face Louise. They entwined their legs and sat, gently stroking each other bodies as they smiled at each other.

"I think we should go on holiday next summer," Louise said, "somewhere hot, just the two of us."

"What? Really?" Mary said, surprised.

"Yes really, we can go and lie around in bikinis in the sun, get drunk, find hot guys, get laid a lot, with them and each other. It'll be great. Fancy it?"

Mary smiled, "I'd love to, but I can't afford anything that extravagant."

"You need a job," Louise said.

"I know, but there's so much coursework to do."

"Then you need a job like mine," Louise said, looking up from running her fingers over Mary's nipples slowly.

"I didn't know you had a job. Where do you work?"

"It's not *really* work, not in my mind. And nobody knows."

"Ok, miss mystery. Spill." Mary said, getting very interested suddenly.

"I escort," Louise said softly, clearly nervous about admitting it to someone she knew.

"You fucking what?" Mary said, stunned.

"I escort. Guys book me, I go out for dinner, or drinks with them."

"You're a prostitute?" Mary said confused.

"No." Louise sniggered a little. "They book me for a dinner date, not for sex."

"So, you don't fuck them?"

"Eww, no," Louise said, "not all of them anyway," she laughed nervously.

"I don't understand?"

"Right, so they book me through an agency, I go out to dinner with anyone who books, and they pay for my time, and the dinner."

"And?" Mary asked, her confusion turning back to interest.

"And I get to decide if that's where the night ends, or if I'm happy to carry on. In which case they pay me, directly."

"For sex?"

"Well, yeah, but you have to be clear on your boundaries, and how much it's going to cost them."

Mary lay there for a second processing it all. She could tell Louise was nervous about the conversation and was clearly in fear of judgement. She sat up, pushed Louise onto her back and straddled her waist, sitting her naked body on Louise's hips. She took her hands and interlocked her fingers in Louise's and rested them on her legs.

"Ok, so, how much does this make?" Mary said softly, smiling down at Louise.

Louise relaxed, realising Mary was in no mood for judgement.

"Well, a 3-hour dinner date, minus the agency commission, earns £300."

"What the fuck?" Mary said, stunned, "why aren't you rolling in money?"

"I only do two or three a month, and after the first few I spent all the money on nice dresses and lingerie and stuff for later dates."

"And how many dates have you had?"

"Seven now."

"And how many of these did you fuck?"

"Two."

Mary looked up to the ceiling, processing the information.

"Hang on, how much did you charge for, you know?"

"Sex?"

"Yeah."

"I don't charge specifically for sex. I give them the choice, £150 per hour for anything that happens after the date, cash. One guy only wanted an hour, the other asked for four."

"And if you don't want to you can just say no and that's it?"

"Of course, the agency knows exactly where you are. You have to text them when you arrive and leave, they have all the client details, and you're in a public restaurant usually, so you just politely decline. I don't have any issues, mostly they are glad to have stared at a smiling young girl in a little black dress for three hours."

Mary let go of Louise's hands and lit a cigarette, still seated on her.

"And why did you fuck those two?" she asked.

"They were hot. It wasn't a hardship. Most of them are older, some a lot older, and mostly businessmen working away, or divorced guys

I think, some widowers, I tend not to ask. It's not my business. You can choose which nights you're available, and how often. The agency is pretty good about it as they can charge more for us, being young and sexy and all. All you need to do is turn up looking a million dollars and smile and chat through dinner."

Mary put finished her cigarette and put it out, then put her hands on Louise's stomach, slowly sliding them upward and cupping her breasts.

"So, let me get this straight. Men will pay me to get dressed up and go on dates with them, then pay for the meals and drinks, then if I want them to, they will pay for sex?"

"Yep."

Mary leaned forward down towards Louise's face and whispered.

"And if I do this, we can go on holiday next summer and I can have your body, and fuck hot guys as often as I like while we're away?"

"Yep."

Mary smiled, "where do I sign up?"

"I'll take you to see Monica tomorrow. She runs it all."

"Mmmm, and how will I ever thank you," Mary said sliding her hand between their entwined legs and stroking Louise's clit. Louise moaned slightly.

"This bed's too small, lie on the floor, I'll show you how to thank me," she said eagerly. Mary climbed off the bed and lay on the rug next to her bed in the small room. Louise climbed off behind her and stood over her, one leg either side of her shoulders, giving Mary a beautiful view of her sex as she tied up her hair. She turned around and knelt, using her legs to press Mary's arms to the floor beside her as she lowered herself close to Mary's mouth.

"Do you have any ideas yet?" She said, giggling a little.

"Lower please." Mary instructed, as Louise lowered herself fully onto Mary's waiting mouth.

Louise looked down as Mary opened her legs and bent her knees at the same time as she pushed her tongue deep inside Louise's wetness.

"I'm going to have to eat something, or I'll make too much noise." Louise said, smiling to herself and buried her face between Mary's legs.

They lay there pleasuring each other for a while before Louise felt an orgasm growing quickly. Her breath went short, and her body started to sweat against Mary's. She knew that she needed to be quiet, but Mary was doing such a fantastic job on her body that she wasn't going to be able to. She lifted her upper body and arched her back, grinding her body down on Mary's mouth aggressively, Mary responded by throwing her arms around Louise's lower back, pulling her down further. Louise alternated between fingering Mary roughly and massaging her clit slowly, which caused her body to start to twitch. Louise could take no more, she moaned loudly and shuddered as she came on Mary's mouth as Mary eagerly lapped up everything Louise's body offered her. Mary, lost in the fun of what she was doing, suddenly realised what her body was telling her, and her legs started to shake violently as Louise continued fingering her as she came too, moaning loudly.

They slowly settled, their breathing returning to normal as Louise slid of Mary's body and lay next to her.

"We need to go on holiday together," Louise said, kissing Mary on the cheek.

"We really fucking do." Mary sighed.

"Reckon we can get away with sharing a shower before bed?" Louise asked.

"It's Friday night in halls of residence, I'm pretty sure we could get away with anything." Mary replied.

They got up and wrapped themselves in towels, then skipped off to the shower together before cuddling up, naked, in bed together. Mary giggled.

"What?" Louise asked.

"Oh, nothing. Just excited for another adventure. And if it gets us away somewhere hot for a few weeks this summer, all the better."

Louise reached up and turned off the light, then kissed Mary goodnight.

Chapter 2

The next morning, Louise was first to wake. She looked at Mary, lying with her back to her as the sun lit the room through the thin curtains, lying asleep with her hair over her face. She traced a pattern down Mary's back with one finger slowly, which had the desired effect. Mary rolled onto her back.

"Morning," Louise whispered.

"Morning," Mary replied.

"Ready to become an escort?"

"Yeah, let's do it," Mary replied confidently.

Louise got out of bed and dressed while Mary lay there having a cigarette. She then called Monica and made an appointment for the two of them to go over to the agency at 11am.

They had some breakfast and caught a train into the city, arriving at the agency a little early. Mary suddenly became nervous.

"What if she doesn't think I'm right for it?" she said to Louise as they stood at the door.

"Mary, take my word for it, she'll want you on the books." Louise said, pulling the door open and guiding Mary inside.

It wasn't a large space. Just a few desks and an office in the corner, and it obviously didn't have any signage outside. But it was in a very upmarket office building. They passed two women taking bookings on the phone at their desks as Louise led Mary to Monica's office and knocked the door.

"Come in!" A friendly voice shouted from behind the door. Louise pushed the door open and led Mary inside.

"Ah, Louise, lovely to see you. Oh, wow, and you must be Mary," Monica said, looking impressed.

She was quite a tall woman attractive woman, in her 50's Mary imagined, and was very warm and welcoming.

"Hi," Mary said sheepishly.

"Mary would like to come onto your books, she's new like me, but I can give her some tips." Louise said.

"Well, Mary, welcome." Monica said, have a seat both.

Over the next half an hour Monica confirmed to Mary pretty much everything that Louise had told her about the evening before. Mary did disclose that she'd only had sex with two men and one woman before and didn't have the amount of sexual experience with men that Louise had, but Monica didn't see it being an issue.

"Hey, you never have to have sex with any of them if you don't want to," Monica said casually, "That's up to you. Beautiful girl like you will get enough offers for bookings and make plenty of money without sex if that's what you want."

Mary completed some paperwork, mostly safeguarding related stuff so they could make sure she was safe, then Monica took a head and shoulders photograph of her, and a full length one. Louise had suggested she wear something nice under her coat for a photograph, and the dress she wore resulted in a photo both she and Monica were more than happy with.

"You use our taxi account to get to and from dates. You must text us when you arrive, and when your date is finished. If you are leaving, tell us, if you are staying, tell us until when then text when you are leaving. Someone will be monitoring the texts at all times, ok?" Monica said, turning very serious, giving Mary some comfort.

"Ok," Mary replied.

"Great, I'll get you listed on the site before lunch." Monica said as Mary put her coat back on. "When are you free? You know, for your first date?"

"Let's just say one night a week to start with," Mary replied, "not bothered which, but not Sundays. Just let me know when and where."

She and Louise left and headed back to university, where Louise collected her belongings and reluctantly left Mary to go to her shared house to do some work. Mary had lunch, then sat at her laptop starting to do some work herself as her phone rang.

"Mary, it's Monica."

"Hi, everything ok?"

"Erm, yes, are you free tonight by any chance?" Monica asked, "We had a booking enquiry for you in less than ten minutes, I think that's a record."

"Wow, really?" Mary said, her heart fluttering a little with nerves.

"Yes, he's a regular, nice guy, no concerns. Wants to take you for dinner in the city."

"Erm, yes, please. I'll take it," Mary replied, slowly closing her laptop. "What time?"

"7pm at The Royal Hotel dining room. We'll confirm your availability with him then one of the girls will text you the final details, ok?"

"Erm, yes, thanks." Mary said nervously.

"Good, best start quickly, and this is quick. Have a good time, I'll call you tomorrow to see how you got on," Monica said, then hung up.

Mary texted Louise, who was equally encouraging and suggested she dress for sex, even if she wasn't planning to offer it. Mary wasn't sure what she meant, so Louise sent her a photo of herself in a short little black dress, low cut at the front, with heels and fishnets from her last escort outing. Mary got the point. She fished out her own little black dress but decided on bare legs and little velvet boots.

Throughout the rest of the afternoon Mary got very little work done. She couldn't concentrate for nerves and excitement, so she had a bath and started to get ready early to make sure she had plenty of time.

The text she received said to ask for *James Morley* when she arrived at the restaurant. She was tempted to do a little online research, but then thought better of it.

When she was dressed, she called a taxi and sat quietly in the back nervously all the way to the city. The taxi dropped her at the hotel at

6:45pm, so she had a cigarette outside, then went into the ladies' toilets and brushed her teeth before collecting up her courage and heading to the restaurant.

When she arrived, the waiter took her date's name and led her across the busy restaurant to a quiet table at the back where a man, presumably James, was waiting.

He stood up and his eyes lit up, as the waiter walked away.

"Hello, you must be Mary," he said, "Wow, you are more beautiful in person than in your pictures."

Mary blushed. "Hello James, nice to meet you," Mary said, as he helped her out of her coat and pulled the chair out for her to sit down.

Mary studied him for a second as he returned to his seat. He was in his forties, she thought, and was wearing a nice blue suit and a well-pressed shirt. He was also reasonably attractive.

"Did you find me ok?" he asked.

"Yes, the taxi dropped me at the door," Mary said as the waiter returned to take a drinks order. Mary looked at him, unsure what to ask for.

"Do you like wine?" James asked.

"Yes, white or rosé though, not red," she replied.

"A bottle of rosé then please." he said to the waiter, who wandered away.

Mary wasn't sure what to talk about, she didn't want to pry into his life any more than she wanted him to pry into hers. Luckily, he was seasoned veteran of the escorting world and kept the conversation light, and they ended up chatting quite freely.

"There's a band on in here later apparently," he said.

"Oh, that'll be nice." Mary said, casting her eyes down to the menu, "Are you a vegetarian?" she asked.

"No," he replied.

"Oh good. Can I order steak then?" Mary asked sweetly, smiling at him.

"Of course, anything you want.," he replied, smiling back.

The waiter appeared with the wine and took their food order while they chatted about the weather, the city, films, practically anything superficial. Mary relaxed, he was a nice guy and she enjoyed talking to him, though she didn't drink much to keep a clear head. She listened attentively, smiling seductively at him frequently and laughing at his jokes. They enjoyed their steaks and had moved on to dessert when Mary started to wonder if he was going to ask for anything extra. As they finished dessert, their table was cleared, and the band started playing at the other side of the room. Mary couldn't remember ever eating at a restaurant this upmarket before, the food was fantastic, the company pleasant, *and* she was being paid to be there – that, she couldn't quite believe.

James hadn't made any effort to come anywhere near her up until this stage, as they had spent the evening sat opposite each other, but eventually he pulled a chair next to him and encouraged Mary to come over and sit with him, claiming it was so that she didn't have her back to the band. She happily went and sat with him. After a few minutes, he looked at his watch.

"I only have forty-five minutes left with you it seems," he said as they watched the band playing.

Mary smiled, "It's been nice though, hasn't it?"

"Dinner with a friendly and beautiful young woman? Yes, my dear, it's been very nice," he replied.

Mary waited. She had a feeling he was about to ask.

"How would you feel about staying a little longer?" he asked.

Mary knew it was coming, but she hadn't mentally prepared for the reality of it, despite the fact he was offering to pay to have sex with her, the offer gave her a bit of a tingle. He wanted her, and she liked that. Right now, she could say no, politely, and leave in a taxi back to university. Alternatively, she could say yes, make some more money and have sex with the older guy sat beside her. And Mary had developed a bit of a thing for older guys after her week with Richard.

"I might be persuaded," she whispered to him, smiling. He put his hand inside his jacket and pulled out a white envelope which he passed to her discreetly.

"How long would this persuade you for?" he asked softly.

She flipped it open and counted, there was around three-hundred pounds in freshly printed twenty-pound notes inside. She'd already decided that Louise was under-pricing herself and she thought her body was worth at least one hundred and fifty per hour.

"Till midnight," she whispered.

"Perfect," he replied, "then you had better put that away."

Mary slipped the envelope into her handbag and put it on the floor beside her. As she did so, and having agreed the 'deal', he was confident enough to place a hand on her knee. Mary knew she'd committed to it now and needed to be his 'girlfriend' until she left. She decided it was time to give him value for all the money he was spending, so turned her legs towards him and crossed them as he caressed them gently under the table, sliding upward very slowly. Her body started to react to him, and she could feel herself becoming aroused, mostly in anticipation, she thought.

As the band stopped for a break, just before ten, he finished his drink and put down his glass. Mary wondered if they were going to go anywhere else, or just staying here watching the band until midnight while he fondled her legs under the table. She got her answer quickly, as he gently squeezed her leg.

"Come on," he said, standing up and holding out a hand for her. She took it and used his strength to pull herself up to stand next to him.

"Where are we going?" she asked, picking up her coat from the back of the chair. "Do I need to put this on?"

"Oh no," James replied. "It's an elevator ride to my room." He said and winked at her. She smiled.

"I just need to let the agency know I'm staying," she said, pulling her phone from her bag. "Give me a sec."

Mary quickly sent a message to the agency mobile saying she would be leaving at midnight, then one to Louise:

'I'm staying later, older guy! leaving at midnight. xxx'

They walked together through the lobby, and he called a lift, they stepped in with another couple, standing behind them. Mary's phone vibrated; it was a reply from Louise. She discreetly looked at it:

'Slut. Enjoy! Full details tomorrow please xx'

The couple in front of them were going to the fourth floor, Mary and James were heading to the ninth. As the doors closed and the elevator started to move, James slide a hand behind Mary and onto her back, she stepped closer to him, encouraging him, so he slid his hand down her back to her rear. They stood there patiently until the other couple got out at their floor and the doors closed.

"Any rules?" James asked, standing next to her looking forward towards the lift doors, his hand still on her rear.

Mary and Louise had talked about this. While in her personal life Mary had very few sexual limits, with *'customers',* no matter how attractive, Louise told her she had to set boundaries – and do it matter-of-factly so as not to offend.

"We use my condoms for penetration and don't come in my mouth or on my face please. Otherwise- "

"-Anal?" James interrupted.

Mary's body and mind screamed YES! at her, she loved anal sex and hadn't done it for too long in her opinion.

"No, sorry," she said reluctantly.

"Don't be sorry," James said, "you should only do what you want to do."

That statement gave her a little comfort.

"And can I kiss you?" he asked as the elevator beeped and the doors opened.

"Anywhere you want to." Mary said as he turned to face her finally. She smiled.

They stood for a second and the elevator doors started to close, distracting James from gazing into her eyes and putting his arm out to stop the doors closing, then stepping out and leading Mary down the corridor to his room. He opened the door and led Mary inside, closing it behind her.

She pulled a couple of condoms from her bag and walked over to the bed, putting them on the bedside table while James hung up their coats. She'd bought some lube, at Louise's suggestion, but she was already quite horny at what she was about to do, so really didn't think she needed to get the out too.

She turned and walked over to him. He stood with his arms by his side. She realised he wanted her to lead, at least to start with so she stepped back from him a little, and slowly pulled her dress over her head, discarding it on the floor. James stood, looking at her body, smiling.

"Show me more." He whispered.

Mary reached behind her back and unclipped her bra, then slid her hands up to the straps and slowly pulled them off her shoulders, allowing her bra to fall to the floor.

"More?" he said.

Mary smiled. She put her fingers on her hips and grasped the sides of her panties gently, then bent forward towards him as she slid them down her legs in one smooth move. They settled on top of her boots, and she stepped out of them gently then stood in front of him, her arms by her sides.

She knew this was a business transaction, but by this stage Mary was so wet she was sure he could sense her arousal.

"You really do have the most beautiful body, Mary," he said.

"Why, thank you kind sir," she replied stepping forward. "Fancy a closer look?"

He put his hand on her shoulders and slowly slid them across her collar bone and down to her breasts as she looked into his eyes. He sighed a happy sigh.

"I think I'm going to enjoy you," he said softly.

"I'm going to make sure you do," Mary replied as she lifted her hands to unbutton his shirt. He slipped his hands from her breasts to her hips while she spent an age teasing him, unbuttoning it slowly. When she had finished with the last button, he took off the shirt and threw it to the floor. Mary slid her hands down his chest and went for his belt, which she again took her time with before opening it and his trousers and letting them fall to the floor. He took them off, kicked off his shoes, and stood in front of her in his underwear. Mary stepped forward and presser her naked body against him, a little to the side, as she slid her hand into his boxer shorts, reaching for his cock. She took it in her hand and gently closed her fingers around it. James let out a gentle sigh.

"Is this for me?" Mary asked, playfully.

"It is," James replied.

"Then you had better take these off and lie down then, hadn't you?"

James took off his boxers, revealing his large, semi-rigid cock and lay on the bed. Mary, still in her boots, climbed on to the bed between his legs on her hands and knees and studied his cock for a second. She was impressed. She looked up the bed at him, his eyes were bristling, clearly anticipating what she was going to do next. Mary maintained eye contact with him as she licked the tip of his cock, then opened her mouth and took it deep inside. James moaned at the feeling of her warm, welcoming mouth around his shaft.

Mary worked his cock for a while, as he lay there smiling with his arms behind his head, until he eventually interrupted her.

"Swap," he said.

Mary slid her mouth off him and lay on the bed as James sat beside her.

"Mind if I?" he said, pointing at her boots.

"Not at all," Mary replied.

He reached down and slowly slid down the tiny zip on the inside of them, pulling each of them off, revealing small black fishnet socks underneath accentuated by red, perfectly painted toenails.

"Wow, these are sexy." He said as he put her boots to one side.

"Glad you like," Mary smiled.

"So sexy in fact, I think I'm going to leave them on."

Slid down the bed and Mary threw one leg over his head, spreading both legs wide, with him sat between them. He stared at her sex, making no secret of it. Mary lay there, enjoying watching his eyes stare into her.

"Your pussy looks perfect," he said, lifting one of her legs and starting to kiss the inside of it from the ankle upward. He took his time, he was paying for it after all, and despite him not being her first choice of sexual partner, Mary was really turned on, by the attention, and the situation.

He didn't immediately go down on her when he reached the top of her leg, instead switching his attention to the other leg and working his way up that too. When he reached the top of that leg however, he could resist his prize no more, and licked Mary's clit slowly.

Mary knew she needed to make noise for him. Louise had said customers like that. But there was no need for any acting right now, there was a warm tongue massaging her clit, and it felt very good. Mary started to moan, then stopped, as James stopped abruptly.

"One sec," he said, reaching for a pillow. "Lift your bum for me."

Mary pressed her feet down on the bed to lift her bottom in the air, as James slid a pillow under the small of her back.

"There we go, perfect. I'll be a while if that's ok?" he asked.

"Take all the time you want," Mary replied, opening her legs a little further.

James slid his fingers slowly across her clit. Mary moaned a little in pleasure. Then he inserted one into her opening, then another, then another, then tugged at her G-Spot. Mary let out a louder moan as her body reacted to his attention. He left his fingers inside her wetness, probing her insides a little as he lay down and re-started his slow a patient attention on her clit with his lips and tongue.

'I can't believe I'm being paid for this.' Mary thought to herself as she closed her eyes, whimpering softly.

After about 15 minutes of James' attention, Mary realised that he had no intention of letting her orgasm. Every time she started to get really excited by what he was doing, he slowed a little, binging her back from the brink. It frustrated her, but she had to keep reminding herself why she was here, and it wasn't for her gratification, no matter how much she was enjoying it. Eventually he raised his head and withdrew his fingers from her body.

He slid up the bed and lay on his side next to her as she closed her legs a little and instinctively reached out to stoke his still rigid cock. He leaned forward to kiss her, as she told him he could. As their mouths met, he slid his tongue into her mouth, and she could taste her own juices on it. She closed her eyes and leaned her body towards him. The kiss was pleasant, but her least favourite activity so far.

"Can I fuck you now?" He whispered, a little more direct that he had been so far.

"Of course!" Mary said. She reached for the condoms on the bedside table and unwrapped one. She sat up and gave his cock a quick shallow suck, before carefully rolling the condom onto him, careful not to damage it with her nails or jewellery. When she was happy, she looked up into his eyes seductively.

"How do you want me?" she asked.

"On your back... ...to start with." He said confidently.

Mary lay back down and opened her legs again as he moved between them and pressed the tip of his cock against her clit. Mary's eyes bristled slightly.

"Give it to me James." She whispered.

"I'm going to," he replied, and quickly slid his cock downward and slammed it into her.

Mary screamed. She wasn't prepared for that to be his opening move. But she was delighted with it. She put her arms up and around his neck as he leaned forward, letting her adjust to the invader inside her body.

"Oh, it's going to be like that is it?" she asked, smiling up at him.

"Yes Mary, it is."

He withdrew to his tip and slammed in again, this time she was expecting it, but still yelped.

He put his arms under her bent knees and lifted them upward, pressing them against her upper body. Mary took her hands from around his neck and held her legs in place for him, wide open, her sex completely exposed to him.

"Ready?" he asked.

"Ready," Mary replied.

Then, for the first time since she met him earlier, she saw his true colours. The pounding Mary's body took was like nothing she had experienced before. He wasn't violent, and she didn't feel at all unsafe, but he was carnal, animalistic, and he was lost in himself – clearly intending on making the most of the opportunity to have her.

"You're so tight around my cock. You feel so fucking good," he said breathlessly, as Mary moaned and yelped with each aggressive thrust into her body. She felt an orgasm building quickly inside her, but it didn't get chance to emerge.

"Roll over," James said, withdrawing quickly.

Mary quickly rolled onto her front, and he yanked her body up onto all fours by her waist.

"Fucking hell your ass is hot," he said from behind her, as she felt his tongue press against her rear opening briefly, which she loved. "You sure I can't fuck it?"

Mary wiggled her bottom at him, teasing. "Yes, I'm sure."

"Ok, well, back to it then," he said, plunging his cock back into her sex from behind.

Mary was used to his technique by now, and quite enjoyed it. She felt like an object, a plaything, a toy for his use, and this ticked a box she'd developed a liking for during her debauched week with Richard. She willed him to finish, to feel as if she'd accomplished her mission. After a few minutes, she got her wish. Without much warning, James went over the edge and slammed into her a couple more times, groaning loudly as she moaned. She imagined the condom filling inside her. She hated them still, but for this 'job' they were a vital ally. Eventually James stopped groaning and held himself inside her for a moment, before slowly pulling out.

Mary turned quickly to check the condom was intact, it was, and it was very full. James wandered off into the bathroom to get rid of it and came back and lay next to her, out of breath still and sweating. Mary glanced at the clock, 11:35pm.

"Thanks Mary. Had a great night, you can get off if you want," he said, smiling at her.

"You sure?" She asked, "you have twenty-five minutes yet, if you want them."

"No, it's fine, I got what I wanted, thanks," he said a little dismissively.

Mary felt she should have been offended at his tone, but instead it turned her on a little.

"Oh, ok, no problem," she said, slipping off the bed and getting dressed.

He sat, still naked but with his back to her on the bed while she dressed, looking at his phone. Once she was ready to leave, she put on her coat and stood waiting. He looked up.

"Bye then, thanks," he said, he still not intending to get up.

"Bye," she replied, and turned and left.

As she walked down the corridor Mary felt torn. On one hand, despite the nice food and the reasonably good sex, she'd been used as a piece of meat and discarded once he'd finished with her, which felt degrading. On the other hand, she'd had nice food and reasonably good sex, then she'd been used as a piece of meat and discarded once he'd finished with her, which really turned her submissive side on. A side that hadn't emerged since Richard left, despite Elliot's best efforts.

As she entered the elevator to head to the lobby, another thought hit her. She'd just made herself six hundred pounds.

She walked through the lobby to the smoking area on the front of the hotel and lit a cigarette while she booked her taxi home. She texted the agency to let them know she was about to leave safely, then just sat happily enjoying her first cigarette all night. She'd just finished it as the taxi arrived, and she climbed in, her pelvis aching slightly from the evening's activities as she sat down and closed the door.

She drifted a little as the car made its way back to campus. She thought about how his manner had reminded her how positively she reacted to being submissive, how she liked that he was older, and was mildly frustrated that despite the sex, she hadn't had an orgasm and was still quite horny, and rather tired.

When the car arrived at campus just after midnight, there were students everywhere. Saturday night on campus meant that at this stage people were either heading home, or to a club, so Mary strolling home in a little black dress didn't look remotely out of place. As she passed the student union she was distracted by a familiar voice.

"Mary?"

It was Elliot her friend with benefits, and closest male friend.

"Hey," she said stopping and giving him a hug.

While she and Elliot shared a bed now and again, he was more than aware than in recent months Mary's growing sexual appetite and curiosity for new experiences meant that he often shouldn't ask too many questions. Ironically, aside from her weeklong sexual liaison with Richard, she'd not actually fully embraced her sexuality yet, and was just getting started.

"How was your date?" he asked.

"What?" she asked quickly, concerned how he could possibly know about her new job and where she'd been tonight.

"With Louise, last night," he said.

Mary relaxed and laughed to herself.

"Fun, lots of fun," she said.

"I bet. Where are you off to?"

"Home, been out, just getting back. You?"

"We're all going clubbing in town. Too tired to come along?"

She didn't have the energy, and despite being only twenty herself, she didn't really appreciate drunk people her own age at all – unless she too was drunk, in which case she found them more tolerable.

"Yeah, sorry, I need my bed," she replied.

"Ok, want some company?" he asked suggestively.

Mary thought for a second. She *was* still horny, and she knew that if she took him back to her room Elliot would to anything she wanted. But that was the problem, he would do anything *she* wanted. Most of the sex they had was like that, and that was great, sometimes, but tonight what she yearned for was not to be given what *she* wanted, it was to be taken, like *he* wanted, and Elliot wasn't the guy for that.

"Thanks, but no, you go on with this lot. I'm going to have a coffee and curl up."

"Ok, see you Monday." Elliot said, kissing her on the cheek.

"Bye," she said quietly, and continued to her room.

When she got back to her room she undressed and put on her dressing gown, then made a coffee and sat on her bed with a cigarette and sent Louise a message.

'Hi, I'm home. x'

'Good. Okay?"

'Yes. x'

'Did you have to close your eyes and think of the money?'

'No, he was pretty good. Nothing earth shattering, but good. Fancy clothes shopping tomorrow? If I'm doing this weekly, I'm going to need plenty of outfits and lingerie.'

'Count me in. I'll come to you at 11?'

'Great, see you in the morning. x'

Mary put her phone down and finished her coffee. Her eyes heavy, she fell asleep on her bed with her dressing gown on.

Chapter 3

Nearly a week had passed since Mary's first outing as an escort. She had received her payment from the agency the morning after the date, so had six hundred pounds to spend on shopping for outfits and lingerie for 'work' as she called it. She didn't spend all of it, but the novelty of having all that money did let her splash out quite a bit.

While they were out shopping, she'd had a detailed review with Louise of her first 'work' date, and a less detailed review on the phone with Monica, who was quite keen for Mary to carry on escorting mainly due to the number of booking enquiries they were getting for her. She was delighted when Mary said she was happy to continue.

On Thursday lunchtime in between lectures, Mary received a call from Monica.

"Hi Monica, do you have one for me?" Mary asked as she answered the call, sat with Louise on a bench on campus.

"Hi sweetie. Yes, I do, in fact you have a waiting list, I'm prioritising regular customers to see you now. This one's a bit strange though."

"Strange how?" Mary asked.

Louise caught her attention and mouthed 'Edward' at her.

"His name's Edward," Monica said. "He's lovely, never asks for the same girl twice, and has never, ever asked for a girl to stay after dinner for anything extra."

"Okay. That's a little strange I suppose," Mary said.

"There's more. He also is very specific about what you should wear and how you should look."

"Go on."

"He likes minimal make up, hair down, and no short skirts. He really likes the girl-next-door look."

"Oh, I can do that, no problem. Anything else?"

"He's sixty. Attractive, but sixty. Louise said you liked older men, but I guess there's a limit?"

"If all I'm doing is going for dinner, it doesn't matter does it, I guess? Of course, I'll take it."

"Wonderful, he's been with us for a while and spends a lot with us, thanks for being accommodating. I appreciate you won't make as much as last weekend, so I'll make it up to you next week. Julie will text you the details tomorrow. He usually arranges dinner earlier, and lives near to the uni campus so you won't need to go into the city this week. Remember, innocent girl-next-door."

"Got it, thanks Monica. Speak soon."

Louise smiled at her as she hung up the phone.

"It's Edward, isn't it?" Louise asked.

"Yes."

"I knew it, I knew he'd want to see you. He's nice, just not into anything more than dinner."

"Do you have a booking this week?" Mary asked.

"Yeah, waiting for details. Saturday night, same as yours. Some Spanish guy in the city for business with a thing for English girls apparently."

"After this weekend and next, I think we should pool some cash and book our holiday." Mary said. "At the rate we're earning we could go anywhere we want to."

"Can't wait." Louise said, grabbing her bag to head back to lectures.

On Saturday morning, Mary got up, had a long pampering bath, then set about becoming the girl-next-door. She'd given it some thought, taking it as a bit of a challenge, and had managed to get into town to do a little shopping on Friday afternoon to make her outfit work. Mindful that the look she was going for would look a little out of place at university, in a hall of residence full of students who knew it wasn't her normal style, she was thankful that rain was forecast, giving her an excuse to leave campus with her hood up.

Dinner had been arranged by her date, Edward, at a restaurant only three miles from campus. At first it seemed a little close for comfort, but Louise rightly pointed out that it was a rather nice upmarket restaurant, and the chances of anyone from university that she knew being in there on a Saturday night was low. He'd booked dinner for five in the afternoon, so she really didn't need to leave until four thirty at the earliest.

After much debate with herself, she had settled on a knee length pale blue pleated skirt, a short-sleeved white blouse with lace on the cuffs and the collar, and white ankle socks with a new pair of black, low heel shoes which almost resembled the kind she used to wear for school.

Much as she pared back her makeup, she still put a little foundation on, and accentuated her eyes a little, but she still looked natural. Finally, she put a cute little blue and white clip in the back of her hair. She even removed her rings and her necklace. She looked at herself in the mirror, proud of her attention to detail.

She took a selfie and sent it to Louise.

'Fuck, do you ever not look hot?' Louise replied almost immediately.

Mary smiled to herself, there was something about this look that made her feel sexy, but in a very different way. It was so different to her current style that it almost felt like role play. She booked the taxi for four thirty to the car park, and wandered across campus in her long coat with the hood up having one last cigarette before she climbed in the back of the car and removed her hood to check her hair was still ok.

Ten minutes later, she arrived at the restaurant and quickly sprayed on a little perfume before climbing out of the car and disposing of the gum she had used to mask the smell of smoke. The restaurant was already quite busy, and she stood in line waiting to speak to the concierge. She looked around the room, keen to see if she could identify her date before being taken to him. She spotted a guy with short silver hair in a pinstriped shirt and black trousers sat side-on to her, sat alone at a table for two. She hoped it was Edward, as he looked quite handsome, for his age.

The diner turned his head and looked at the queue and his eyes met Mary's. She smiled pleasantly, and the diner beamed from ear to ear. She blinked, he blinked back.

"Yes miss?" The concierge said, breaking her silent conversation with the diner.

"Edward Mills?" She said, he's expecting me.

"Ah, yes. He said. Do follow me please."

Mary followed the man across the room straight to the man she'd been exchanging glances with.

"Hello Mary." Edward said, standing up as she came over.

"Hello Edward," she said, leaning in and letting him kiss her on the cheek. The concierge took her coat and Edward pulled out a chair for her, next to him rather than opposite, and she sat down.

He sat down next to her and poured her a glass of water.

"You look pretty," he said.

'Pretty', Mary thought to herself. 'I need to play up to this age thing, might be fun.'

"Thank you," she replied, feigning embarrassment, "I wanted to look my best for you."

"I appreciate that. Too many young girls your age want to show all their flesh and cover themselves in make-up. It's not ladylike."

'If only you knew' she thought.

"I agree," she said.

The waiter came over to take their drinks order. Before Mary could pick up the menu, Edward spoke.

"A small white wine for me please, I'm driving. You'll have?"

Mary decided to go all out innocent.

"An orange juice please," she said.

Edward looked delighted. In that moment Mary's suspicions were confirmed and she knew exactly how to play the rest of the evening.

"What are you having for dinner?" she asked him, looking at the menu.

"Garlic mushrooms, then a filet steak, then probably something light. You?" he asked.

She studied the menu for a moment, she'd happily eat anything on there.

"Why don't you choose for me," she said, putting the menu down and smiling at him and gently placing a hand on his for a second. He smiled as she withdrew her hand and placed it back in her lap.

"I would be more than happy to my dear," he replied.

As the enjoyed their dinner together, Mary continued to size him up. While they were eating their mains, he continually watched her as she ate, and even at one point insisted on arranging her napkin in her lap to ensure she didn't get peppercorn sauce on her skirt. She concluded that this wasn't a daddy-daughter kink, as she initially thought. For him it was dominance versus innocence, experience versus naivety, though in creating that an element of age-play came into it. Mary enjoyed playing up to it, as 'submissive Mary' awoke inside her once more.

She started to act a little bit silly occasionally, dropping something, or asking for help cutting something on her plate. Every little thing she did he responded to eagerly, and she was curious about what had bought them together. Eventually she had to shed the façade for at least a short while to have a reasonable conversation.

"So, you don't like the other girls you have met?" she asked.

"I don't know what you mean," he replied.

"Monica told me you have never seen the same girl twice," she whispered.

"Oh, that. No, I haven't. Not yet," he whispered back.

"And you live nearby?"

"Yes, just a mile from here, on the Anbury estate."

Mary put down her cutlery and stared at him.

"You live on *the* Anbury estate?", she said in her normal voice, forgetting the sweet and innocent one she'd been using so far.

"I do," he said softly.

Mary had been through it once. It was a rite of passage for all new local University students to walk down the single private road that was lined with mansions from one end to the other. It was like a field trip to see what a successful student could achieve. There was a house there that didn't cost millions.

"Wow," she whispered to herself, picking up her cutlery and trying to get back into character.

"Please tell me you have a pool?"

Edward laughed, "Yes, I have a pool."

Mary concluded that none of the other girls he had met knew he was almost definitely a millionaire, as Monica would almost definitely know it and would have told her.

"I'd love to see your house sometime," she whispered softly.

He looked as if he was about to say something as the waiter returned to clear their plates and broke the conversation, asking about dessert. Edward ordered for both of them, as he had all evening, and the waiter disappeared. Not wanting to push too much, Mary sat twiddling her spoon and smiling at Edward, who studied her curiously.

"You are a little sweetie, aren't you?" he said.

'Not at all' she thought.

"I try," she said, as the waiter put a lemon sorbet in front of each of them.

They finished their dinner and chatted over coffee, superficially, until just before eight. Edward looked at his watch.

"Time's up," he said, looking a little disappointed. "It's been lovely, you have been lovely Mary, thank you."

"It was my pleasure Edward," she replied in her sweet, soft voice. "It's a shame we won't meet again."

Again, he looked like he wanted to say something, but stopped himself. The waiter arrived with the bill and their coats.

After Edward paid, he walked Mary to the door and out into the late afternoon sunshine, the rain having receded.

"Oh, silly me, I need to book my taxi," Mary said as they stood in front of the restaurant. She reached into her handbag and pulled out her phone.

"Did..." Edward started.

She looked up at him. "Sorry?"

"Did you want to see the house?" he asked a little nervously. Then I could drop you straight back home.

"That would be lovely Edward, thank you." She said, clicking her heels sweetly.

"I, I don't have any cash on- "

"We're just going along to look at the house, yes?" she asked.

"Oh, yes, absolutely. That's all." He said confidently, almost as if not wanting to offend her.

"Then you don't need any cash, Edward," she replied. Let's go.

They walked over to his car, a large, new, very expensive looking BMW, and they climbed in. As he drove the short distance to his house, Mary studied him. He hadn't made the slightest effort to make physical contact with her all evening, despite her feeling a little sexual tension. He seemed comfortable with her around, and really responded well to being able to at least feel like he was looking after her.

As they drove onto the estate, Mary tried to guess which of the houses was his. Having only been down here once, she didn't remember much about the houses, other than their size. About halfway down the private road, he turned left towards a gate, which slowly slid back as they sat there waiting, and he pulled in front of what Mary could only describe as a mansion.

"Wow," she said, speaking for the first time since they left the restaurant.

He stopped and took off his belt and looked at her.

"I was lucky, built a business someone else wanted to buy. Sold it for a fortune."

"Do you live with anyone?" she asked curiously. Not really thinking it might be considered nosey.

"No, my wife died five years ago, not long after we bought the place. I've been here on my own ever since. It was her dream home, so I don't feel I can sell it and downsize," he said quite openly.

"I'm sorry," Mary said genuinely.

"Don't be. I'm happy here. I have some good friends, and occasionally I take a pretty girl out for dinner," he smiled, trying to lift the conversation a little, "shall we go in?"

"Let's," Mary said, eagerly.

As they entered the house and he closed the door behind them, Mary was in awe.

"Go on," he said, "take a look around, I'll go and make coffee, want one?"

"Are you sure?" she asked.

"Yes of course, it's just a house. I'll meet you in the kitchen. Latte again?"

"Please," Mary replied as he strolled off through a door at the back of the hall.

In front of her was a grand looking staircase which led to the first floor, then above It another heading to the second. She walked around the hall, her heels clicking as she looked through each door in turn. There was an office, a huge dining room, multiple lounges, a bathroom, a library, it just went on and on. She went up the staircase and bedroom after bedroom, all with ensuite bathrooms, all made up and ready for use. On the top floor she found Edwards room. It had to be, she thought, as it was the only one that looked lived in. It was huge and took up the whole top floor of the house with its walk-in wardrobes, dressing room, balcony to the back garden, and large wet room.

Eventually she made her way back down to the door he had disappeared through in the hall and arrived in a large kitchen with an even larger conservatory attached to it, flooded with light. Edward was sitting on a sofa in the conservatory, having made their drinks.

"Edward!" she exclaimed as she walked across the kitchen toward him, "This is unbelievable."

He laughed. "Thanks Mary. I forget, I've got used to it really."

Mary, keeping in character, stood at the sofa opposite him, took off her coat and sat down. She put her knees to one side, keeping them close together and put on hand on each. She saw his reaction, he loved it. She smiled at him and reached out and picked up her coffee from the table.

"I'll show you the pool when you have had your coffee. Saves it getting cold." he said.

Mary sat looking around, still in awe.

"Mary, can I say, thank you," he said.

"For what?" she asked.

"I know you have put on an act for me this evening. And even after our time ran out you have kept it up for me. I really appreciate that."

Mary smiled. "It comes naturally to me, believe it or not," she said, dropping the act briefly and talking normally. "It wasn't too long ago I *was* the innocent girl sat in front of you. I didn't start to know much of the adult world till university, and even now I am still learning. And besides, I quite enjoy it."

"Acting?" he asked.

"No, *this* act," she replied, smiling at him.

"Would you like to see the pool?"

"Ooh, yes please," she replied, switched back to her sweeter, softer voice.

Edward held out a hand across the coffee table and she took it, allowing him to help pull her back to her feet. She didn't let go and allowed him to lead her across the back of the conservatory and to another door. He opened it and she let go of his hand and went through into the next room. It was a huge room with a glass atrium bathing light onto the swimming pool. At one end there was a hot tub and scattered around it were a few chairs and loungers.

Mary nearly swore but kept in character.

"If only I had my costume." she said cheekily. "It's amazing."

"There's a sauna over there and a gym and some changing rooms." Edward said, pointing to a row of doors at the back of the room. Mary couldn't quite believe it. She looked to her left through the windows and could just see a huge tree-lined lawn heading away from her.

She shook her head at him, "amazing. I'm running out of words. I bet you spend half your life cleaning."

Edward laughed. "No, I have a housekeeper, two cleaners, a man looks after the pool area, and two gardeners."

"Do you have an army of servants in the basement too?" she asked laughing.

"No, there's just room for my garage under the house, and the boilers and a few other things," he said, almost sounding defensive.

She turned and followed Edward back through the door and into the conservatory once more.

"Would you? Swim I mean," he asked.

"Of course! I love swimming," she replied.

She went to pick up her coat and he sat back on the sofa opposite, frowning for a second.

"Mary, come and sit for a minute," he said, patting the sofa next to him. She put her coat back down and went and sat next to him, back straight, knees together, hands on them again, looking at him.

"You can drop the act a minute, I want to ask you something."

She sat back in the chair, relaxing for the first time all evening. Curious about what was coming next.

"What's on your mind?" she asked.

"How would you feel about a separate arrangement to your agency work? Just come around during the day at weekends and spend time with me here. I'd buy you all the clothes you want for when you are here, you could have the run of the place. I know you have university work to do, so you could do that here too if you wanted, and you're still free to live your life outside this house however you wanted to, with the agency, boyfriends, whatever, just never mention any of it here to maintain the act. Obviously, I'd pay you."

He looked timid, embarrassed. She wanted to give him a hug and tell him it was ok to ask but she didn't. He looked out of the window, waiting for an answer. Mary studied him. The offer seemed genuine enough and was quite appealing. She wouldn't find it hard to spend time here with him, he was a nice guy, in a *much* older, good-looking, slightly dominant way. Mary's inner submissive was screaming at her to accept.

"What are you doing Wednesday afternoon?" she asked.

"He turned back quickly to look at her. "Nothing, why?"

"I have Wednesday afternoons off lectures. Book me with Monica and take me out for a late lunch. I'll have an answer then. I just want to think it through first. Okay?"

He smiled. She knew he'd like her being unsure and need to think about it rather than rushing in.

"I'll do that," he said, "I had better get you home."

Mary stood and put on her coat, while he collected his car keys from the kitchen worktop. They sat in silence on the short ride back to campus. A comfortable silence, which they both enjoyed.

As he pulled up at the car park, Mary scanned around for anyone she knew who might see her. It was dark being nearly nine-thirty and the campus was still quiet while hundreds of students got ready to go out. She looked across at him.

"Thank you, Edward. This was lovely. I'll see you on Wednesday?" she said, blinking at him sweetly.

"Thanks Mary, yes, you will."

She climbed out of his car and waited until he was out of sight to light a cigarette, as she was sure good girls don't smoke and he wouldn't approve.

She was quite excited by Edwards proposition, and wanted to talk to Louise about it, but couldn't as she knew she was out on a date herself, so she retrieved a bottle of wine from the fridge when she got back to her room and flopped onto the bed with a glass of wine and a box of chocolates.

She spent the rest of the evening scribbling down ideas and thoughts on his suggestions, trying to see if she could make it work. Psychologically she really responded to the caring older man keeping her sweet and innocent. Especially if it was paying for her to go on holiday with Louise and be anything but sweet and innocent. The multi-million-pound mansion with a pool was just a bonus.

She and Louise had already arranged to meet for breakfast the next morning, and they sat in the coffee shop while Louise first told Mary all about the wealthy Spanish businessman she'd been out with last night. Louise had been on a standard 7pm – 10pm date, but the Spaniard had offered her £300 for 3 hours alone in his hotel room, which Louise had happily taken and had really enjoyed the sex.

Mary slowly told Louise all the details of her date with Edward, the trip back to his house, and his proposal. Louise sat open mouthed by the time Mary had finished.

"So, hang on, Edward's a millionaire, and he wants to pay you to come to his mansion and swan around like a young innocent girl. How young exactly?" Louise said, clearly a little bit concerned, despite having had dinner with him herself last month.

"Legal Louise," Mary replied sternly, defending him a little, "I'm only just twenty myself."

"I had a feeling he'd like you. You do sweet and innocent just as well as you to slutty and easy."

"It's a gift," Mary said, laughing.

"You are going to do it I assume?"

"I'd be mad not to. He's happy for me to still escort and do whatever I want outside of being at his house, and with him and Monica's money, we could go somewhere *really* exotic next summer."

"Or just stay for longer," Louise said.

"Or both!" Mary replied, getting excited.

Louise looked out of the window. "I presume there will be sex?" she asked.

"Maye, but there's been no sign yet at all."

"He's mad. I want to fuck you every time I lay eyes on you," she said, smiling.

"I know exactly what you mean," Mary replied, stroking the back of Louise's hand gently on the table. "Have you got much on today?"

"Work, tons of it, essay to write," Louise replied.

"Me too, shall we go to the library and do it together. We can fuel up on coffee and work till it's done then treat ourselves later?"

"To what?" Louise asked, raising an eyebrow.

"Takeaway, wine, trashy TV, and sex." Mary whispered.

Louise smiled and turned her hand over under Mary's so she could hold it. "How could I possibly refuse an offer like that? I'll nip home and get my books."

Chapter 4

Monica rang Mary on Monday, both curious and surprised to have had a call from Edward asking to see Mary again and suggesting it had been pre-arranged with her for Wednesday lunchtime. She did try to get details, but Mary simply said they had a good time and he asked to see her again. From the conversation Mary was entirely confident that nobody at the agency had realised his address when he registered his details with them, so nobody other than Mary and Louise knew his background. He'd asked for a two-hour booking for lunch, which Mary agreed, and Monica went away as normal to set things up and send her the details.

Later that afternoon Mary received the text with the details in. Edward had asked for her to attend a restaurant on a lake in a country park a few miles away, and at the bottom he'd simply requested that she 'dress similar'.

On Wednesday, armed with the slip of paper she'd prepared with prompts on, she called a taxi and headed out to the restaurant. As she walked through the door, her eyes quickly found his. He was sat at a table overlooking the water. She watched him look her up and down, then melt. She pointed him out to the waiter who let her through to come to him by herself.

She wore a full-length white cotton skirt, and a light pink blouse, with white pumps. She felt good if she was honest, despite looking like she was on her way to church, and she loved the way the skirt swayed around her as she walked towards him.

He went to stand but she put her hand out and gestured for him to remain seated, she walked around the table, put her hands on his shoulder gently, then leaned down and kissed his cheek.

"Hello Edward," she said softly, taking her seat.

"Mary, you look lovely."

"Thank you, it's new, I bought it especially for lunch. Have you ordered?"

"No, not yet. What would you like?"

Mary didn't even pick up the menu.

"Will you order for me again please? You make such good choices," she said, and blinked at him. He liked that.

"Of course."

A short while later, they were sat with salads and soft drinks in front of them. They were chatting away about the lake, and the boats, and the weather. While talking a lot, they were generally not saying anything at all, but they were both comfortable. Eventually, after their plates had been taken away and they were sat with coffee, Edward bought up the conversation they needed to have.

"So, any thoughts on my offer?" he asked quietly.

"Lots of thoughts." Mary said happily. "I've got some ideas, mind if I?" she asked, pulling the slip of paper from her bag.

"Not at all, I'm all ears." Edward said curiously.

Mary cleared her throat.

"So, I can do one day every weekend during term time, it may have to alternate between Saturday and Sunday depending on what I'm doing. I'm thinking ten in the morning till about nine in the evening. I'll need to do my university work sometimes, like we said on Saturday, and that has to be a priority, though I am happy to do it at your house."

She paused for a second.

"Done," he said calmly. "And?"

"And if it's ok, I'll need a bedroom. Obviously, I won't be staying over, but I'll be happier if I can change when I get to your house to wear the things you like. So, a room with a wardrobe where I can keep things would be useful." She paused again.

"Still good." Anything else?

"Not really, other than needing to keep this completely separate from my real life, and the financial arrangement," she said, feeling awkward bringing up the subject of money.

"My turn then?" he asked quietly.

"Oh, yes please. Sorry," she said.

"Don't apologise. It's fine."

"Ok."

"So, you can have your own room. You can have a key for it, so you can be assured of privacy when you want it. You can keep anything you like at my house in your room, so you don't have to bring things every time you come over. You can work anywhere you want to, my office, the garden, the kitchen, I don't mind. Your university work is important."

Mary smiled.

He reached into his jacket pocket and put a gold credit card on the table in front of her.

"This is for clothes, taxis, and anything else you need to bring to my house. It has a one-thousand-pound limit, which I'll pay off each month. It's only for things to do with our arrangement though, ok?"

Mary shuddered in shock.

"Ok," she whispered, unable to believe what was happening.

"When you arrive each time, I'll keep out of the way until you emerge from your bedroom, so I don't see you in your normal clothes. I only ever want to see *my* Mary."

"Ok," she whispered again, processing everything.

"We can iron out any other details as we go, but the detail you most likely want to know is this," he said, putting a folded piece of paper on top of the credit card.

"This is for ten in the morning until nine in the evening, one day each weekend during term time.

She picked up the slip of paper and opened it. Her eyes glistened, she smiled a little, then put it back down and looked across at him.

"Eleven hours of your time at Monica's rates would cost me more than that, and you would get less. So, this seems fair. It'll go in your account the morning after each day you spend with me."

"A thousand pounds a month?" she whispered.

"No Mary, that's per visit. I know the girl sitting in front of me isn't you, and I know the time and effort you have put into meeting me and the façade you have to act out, And, you have done it twice for me now. That means a lot and is worth recognising. We will never, ever speak of money again unless we really need to. I just need to know if you are happy with this?"

'Four thousand pounds a month.' Mary thought to herself excitedly. *'And a clothes budget!'*

"I'm yours," she said softly.

He smiled as she slowly picked up the credit card and put it in her purse.

"The pin number is on the back of the slip of paper I gave you."

Mary smiled and picked it up, putting it with the credit card.

He passed her a pen and a piece of paper.

"Bank details please," he said calmly.

Mary fished her phone from her bag and opened her banking app, scribbling down her details for him. Then wrote her phone number underneath.

"Helps if you can text or call."

He smiled.

"That reminds me," he said, reaching down to the floor next to him and passing her a box wrapped in plain white wrapping paper. "This is a little gift for you."

She looked at it excitedly.

"Can I open it here?"

"Please do."

She turned it over and slowly teased the wrapping paper open, revealing a brand new, top of the range iPhone.

"Yours looked like it had seen better days. That screen is in a right state," he said.

Mary's face lit up.

"Your sim will fit it, just slot it in and set it up."

"I don't know what to say, thank you," Mary said happily.

"You're very welcome," he said, passing her the paper carrier bag he'd bought it in. She popped it inside and put it with her handbag.

"So, Saturday? I'll need to use this card quickly to get me started."

"I'll text you my address, go online and get anything you need delivered to my house, use overnight delivery if you want. I'll put everything in your room for you to sort when you arrive."

Mary could tell he was really enjoying spoiling her.

"I'll do that, thank you," she said, finishing her coffee.

"So, that's all the awkward conversations out of the way. Wasn't too painful," he said, mostly to himself.

Mary put her hand on the table and saw him look at it. She could tell he wanted to touch it, hold it, but he didn't.

"I'd better get back and do some shopping then," she said happily.

"Would you like a lift?" he asked.

"Probably best not. A student arriving on campus with a handsome older guy in an expensive BMW in the middle of the day raises eyebrows," she replied, laughing.

Mary booked a taxi on Monica's account and they went outside. She gazed across the car park at a black Aston Martin parked facing them.

"Wow, that's pretty" she whispered under her breath as the taxi pulled up in front of them.

"Yeah, I didn't bring the BMW today," Edward said, clicking his remote and the lights on the Aston coming on. Mary laughed.

"Seriously?"

"I'll take you for a ride in it sometime, see you Saturday at ten," he said, kissing her on the cheek and strolling away.

Mary climbed into the taxi and watched as he opened the door to the Aston. She looked down into her lap and shook her head in disbelief, smiling to herself as the taxi pulled away.

When she arrived on campus, mindful of her outfit, Mary did up her long coat, after folding up the skirt so it didn't show beneath and moved quickly across campus back to her room. She was happy that she wouldn't need to keep doing this when she had her room ser up at Edwards house.

She made a coffee, put her new iPhone on charge, lit a cigarette, and fired up her laptop for an afternoon of online shopping. Before she could start, she received a text from Edward with his address, and telling her to use the same address for the cardholder. She smiled.

'Glad he mentioned that,' she thought.

She didn't reply, consciously, keeping a slight air of mystery and trying not to look too available for him, and set about shopping.

It took hours and cost a small fortune. She ordered shoes, pumps, socks, skirts, dresses, tops, panties, bras, tights, hair accessories, leggings, bodysuits, swimwear, and a few jumpers. When she was satisfied she had finished, she sat at her desk and brushed her hair, then looked at the brush and sighed. She opened her laptop once more, and ordered a hairbrush, toothbrush, toothpaste, perfume, deodorant, razors, moisturisers, make-up, the list was endless, but she wanted to make sure she could just arrive and everything she needed would be in her room.

She got a real kick out of choosing all the clothes. She'd modelled everything on a young innocent look, and couldn't wait to try some of her outfits, though she would have to wait for Saturday. She picked up her old phone then texted him.

'Wardrobe version one ordered, lots coming to your house, sorry!'
'Don't be, look forward to seeing it. See you Saturday.'

She spent the rest of the afternoon setting up her new phone, then got ready for student night, slipping back to her normal self and selecting an outfit for the evening Edward would most certainly not approve of, which secretly amused her.

She headed out and met up with Louise and the rest of their friends at the student union. She had been quite horny for a few days, inexplicably considering how plutonic her week had been, which she put it down to the *'Edward effect'.* Feeling wanted, but not wanted at the same time, by an older man, was doing something peculiar to her.

In any case, having chatted with Louise through the arrangements, and being completely jealous at the whole thing, Louise went looking for Nathan – an occasionally hook-up of hers, and Mary decided that she'd neglected Elliot for a while, so tonight his luck was in.

Having had a few vodkas with Louise, she located Elliot playing pool with a group of his friends from the football team. She wandered over and strolled up behind him.

"Boo," she whispered in his ear. He turned and looked at her.

"Hey sexy," he said.

"Hi," she replied smiling up at him.

"Coming clubbing?" he asked.

"Maybe," she replied, "unless I get a better offer."

Elliot didn't need any further information.

"Your place?" he asked.

"It's closer than yours."

"When?"

"I'm drinking some more. Find me at eleven," Mary replied.

"I certainly will do," he said, as she turned and walked away from him, her short dress drawing his attention to her long slim legs. He snapped out of it and returned to the pool table.

"I can't believe that's the same sweet, innocent Mary you deflowered last year. Fuck she's changed," his friend Brian said, also watching her wander away.

"Yeah, just a bit," Elliot said, almost proudly.

"She's incredible, I'd hand over a year's student loan for an hour alone with her."

Elliot had been through a bit of a rollercoaster with Mary. From initially being a couple, to him taking her virginity, to them both settling on being fuck-buddies rather than a couple, then her turning into an insatiable nympho after her submissive week at the hands of Richard last month. He had a lot of interesting sex stories he could share with his friends, but he felt lucky to be a part of her life, and she trusted him, so he kept his stories to himself. He just smiled occasionally when one of his friends lusted after her in his presence.

About an hour later, having watched Mary from across the room doing her best to finish off all the vodka in the student union, Elliot strolled casually way from his friends and over to her as the mass exodus of students to the nightclubs in town began.

"Ah, here you are," Mary said, finishing her last drink and standing in front of him. She put her hands around his neck and pulled him close so she could whisper in his ear.

"Take me to my room and fuck me, Elliot."

Eliot picked up her coat and helped her put it on as Louise sidled over with Nathan and put her arms around Mary. They hadn't been affectionate in public before, and even with the alcohol Mary was a little taken aback by Louise's public display of affection.

"Have a nice night my beautiful girl," Louise whispered, leaning forward and kissing Mary in front of their 'dates'. Mary put her arms around Louise, lost in the kiss for a moment. Eventually Louise pulled back and looked up at Elliot, while she still held Mary.

"Fuck my girls brains out for me, Elliot," she whispered to him. "If you can manage it."

Louise knew that Elliot wasn't the type, as did Mary. She also knew that if Mary was horny enough, she would do all the work herself, which would do, for tonight.

She hugged Mary and let go of her, turning to Nathan.

"Come on, you have work to do," she said, taking his hand and almost dragging him from the room. Mary and Elliot laughed, then she turned to him.

"Come on, you have me to do," she whispered much more quietly.

They quickly made their away across campus back to Mary's room. She went off to the toilet quickly while Elliot turned on the lamp and cleared her laptop and dressing gown from her bed. When she returned, Elliot was sat on her desk-chair in the dim light. He gave Mary an idea.

She held out a hand, which he took, and she pulled him to his feet, then slowly opened each button on his shirt, pulling it open for him to discard on the floor. He reached for her dress, and she batted his hand away.

"No," she said firmly.

She stepped forward once more, undid his belt and pulled down his jeans and boxer shorts, then stroked his soft but growing cock briefly before pushing him back into the chair. She collected the belt from her dressing gown and tied his wrists together, then tied the spare belt to the back of the chair. He could have escaped easily enough, but Elliot got the point.

She knelt in front of him and took off his shoes, pulled off his jeans and underwear then stood back up to look at him.

"Change of plan," she said. "I'm going to fuck *your* brains out."

She reached down between his legs and cupped his balls, then slid her nails slowly along the length of his now fully erect manhood. He sighed in pleasure.

Mary stepped back another step, then slowly peeled off her dress. She hadn't been wearing a bra, so stood in front of him in a thong and her heels. He looked at her body longingly. She liked that, a lot.

Next, she slowly slipped her thong down to the floor and stepped out of it. Elliot subconsciously licked his lips at the sight of her shaven sex. He clearly wanted to taste her. She slid a hand down to her clit, making herself moan a little as she stood in front of him, before sliding a finger inside herself. She withdrew it and placed it on his lips, and he eagerly sucked it clean.

By this stage Mary was too horny for words. Fuelled with vodka, and filled with confidence, she stepped over to her bed and collected a bottle of lube and her vibrator, placing then on the desk next to him. She stepped forward and straddled him, impaling her sex onto his cock s she allowed her weight to rest on his lap. She sat still, with his cock inside her, staring at him with a beaming smile on her face.

"Ok?" she asked.

"Very," Elliot replied sheepishly.

She put one hand behind his neck and leaned back as he took her weight, then with the other hand she picked up her vibrator, turned it on, and placed it on her clit while she moaned and slowly rode his cock.

Elliot realised she was using him. He wasn't complaining, but he knew that what was happening was a reaction to something, or someone else. He'd seen this from her before.

She dug her heels into the carpet and used her legs to slowly raise and lower her pelvis onto him while the vibrator quickly raised her body temperature. She moaned louder and louder and Elliot half expected her to have an orgasm sat in his lap. Then she abruptly stopped and tossed the vibrator onto her bed. Elliot looked confused.

"Not yet," she whispered. She stood up and turned her back to him, her heels keeping her rear at eye height for him, she stepped back and straddled the chair once more, bending over and putting her hands on his knees. Her sex glistened in front of his face, as she slowly rocked backwards, allowing him to taste it. He slid his tongue inside her, much to her pleasure and started to probe around as much as he could within the confines of his makeshift restraints. She ached her back slightly, and he took the opportunity to run his tongue upward and across her rear opening. She twitched in acceptance and pushed back a little, allowing his tongue to probe her rear a little deeper. She let him carry on for a while, as she panted and moaned, then she stepped forward and picked up the lubricant. She poured a little into the palm of her hand, then dipped her fingers in it, slid her hand down her back, and massaged it into her rear slowly, inches from his face.

Elliot was thrilled. They'd done it a few times in the last month or so, but never quite as erotically as this.

Mary walked around behind him and released his wrists from the chair.

"Do you know what I want, Elliot?" she asked seductively.

"Yes," he whispered.

"Good," she said.

She climbed onto the bed on all fours and lowered her upper body onto her elbows, raising her shapely rear upward invitingly. Elliot stood on the bed between her legs, then squatted down over her waiting body.

"Ready?" he asked.

"Don't ask, just do," she said sharply.

He pressed his cock against her opening and with very little resistance he slid into her behind a little. Mary moaned.

"Don't stop till you're finished," she insisted, brushing her hair from her face and exposing a rather hungry, desperate expression.

"Finished?"

"Finished."

She'd never done this with him before. Previously she had preferred him to pull out and finish on her body, but this was an instruction she'd clearly given advance thought to.

He grabbed her hips and pulled her body backward, impaling her onto his full length.

"Holy fuck. Yes, Elliot do that, do that more."

He withdrew and cheekily pressed in hard, to give her a little of what she said she wanted. To his surprise his action was met with more encouragement, so he continued fucking her, hard by his standards.

Ironically, to Mary this wasn't as vigorous as she would have liked. Elliot was sweet and didn't have that carnal instinct that made him want to take her body aggressively. Since Richard, she had ached for it, but neither Elliot nor her first escort date – the only two men she'd had sex with since Richard left – gave her what she yearned. This however, was more than hot enough for now and Elliot was trying, bless him.

He pounded away at her rear for a few minutes then started to tense. This bit, he *could* do right. Mary became really excited as Elliot started to groan.

"I'm going to come," he said, almost as if giving her one last chance to change her mind.

"Do it, do it now," she panted.

He gripped her hips hard and slammed into her – ironically the first time he'd done it as hard as she'd have liked – as he drained himself into her body. Mary loved every second of it, as Elliot pressed harder and harder into her as his come flowed into her behind. Eventually he settled and withdrew, leaving Mary on all fours with her ass in the air while he stepped off the bed. She allowed herself to slowly return to normal – her rear slowly closing to its normal state, before lying on her side, her eyes glistening as she held his come inside her.

"Thanks Elliot. I needed that," she said, reaching for a cigarette. Elliot pulled on his underwear and looked at her lying there naked. He glanced at his watch.

"You have time to get to the club if you like," she said.

"You sure? I thought this was an all-nighter?"

She laughed. "No, too much vodka, I'll be asleep in half an hour. You go on, have fun."

Elliot was now entirely sure he'd been used. But he still didn't mind. He started to put on his clothes.

"What's the deal with you and Louise?" he asked.

"What do you mean, deal?" she replied.

"You seem to be getting pretty close. Like more than friends close."

"If you're asking if we're having sex, then yes we are," Mary said calmly.

"I was asking if it's more than sex."

Mary thought about Louise for a second and her heart fluttered a little.

"Maybe it is, maybe it isn't," she said.

Once Elliot was fully dressed, Mary stood up to see him to the door.

"Oh, by the way, Brian said he'd pay you a whole year's student loan to have sex with you," Elliot said, laughing a little.

"A whole year? I couldn't possibly charge him that much," she said.

Elliot had no idea there was truth in that statement, which amused her.

"Thanks then," he said. "I'll see you at lectures tomorrow afternoon."

"You will," she replied, reaching up and kissing him briefly before strolling back to her bed, kicking off her heels and lying back down, still naked.

He stepped out into the corridor and closed the door, shaking his head in disbelief a little as he headed off into town.

Chapter 5

Mary had refused an offer from the agency for a date on Friday night, having been out in the week with Edward. Monica was fine with it, as she'd technically done two dates last week and she stalled Mary's growing queue of customers to the following week, on the basis that Mary agreed to at least one.

Mary had decided to make herself available to the agency on Wednesdays, at least for now. Student nights weren't really ticking her boxes, she didn't have lectures on Wednesday afternoons or Thursday mornings, and she could easily get off campus dressed up on Wednesdays as everyone else was. It also meant that she could be rested and prepared to go to Edwards on Saturdays.

She felt a little guilty about the Edward situation, as it was an arrangement Monica had facilitated but she and Edward had taken to one side, so she was keen to carry on with the agency for a while to allay her guilt a little. She also liked the effect it was going to have on her bank balance, and she desperately wanted the holiday abroad that Louise had suggested next summer.

On Saturday morning, Mary woke up very early, and had a bath, then texted Edward.

'Hi, I'll be with you by 10 if still ok?'

'Hello. Yes. Looking forward to seeing you.'

'Great! I have something here to wear for today. Won't need to change in a hurry.'

'No problem. Lots of parcels here to open. I have put them in your bedroom. Did you order a hairdryer for all that beautiful hair?'

Mary smiled, then sighed and looked at the ceiling. She hadn't ordered a hairdryer or any straighteners.

'No, I forgot. I will have to ring mine from here.'

'No, don't. Write down what you want, and I will go shopping for you when you get here. You can have some time getting used to being in the house and sorting your room.'

Mary smiled. He was looking after her again. She typed thank you, then added a single kiss on the end.

'You're welcome, see you at 10. x'

He added a kiss too. Mary smiled and put her new phone carefully to one side while she got ready.

As winter was closing in, she had chosen a long black gypsy skirt and a black roll neck jumper to go to his house. It wasn't quite the look she'd spent hours designing on Wednesday afternoon, but all of that new clothing was waiting for her at the mansion she was about to head over to, so this would do, for this morning at least. She went with the school-ish shoes and white ankle socks rather than her knee-high boots, as this seemed to lower the age of the look somewhat. She pulled up her hair in a tight ponytail, and put very little make-up on, before calling her taxi at around 9:30.

On the way over, she started to get a little excited. She knew she had to fall into her act when she arrived, and this was purely a non-sexual business arrangement, but the dynamic between them *really* ticked her boxes.

When she arrived, she strolled over to the door and took a deep breath before ringing the bell. A moment later, Edward opened the door and smiled down at her. He looked quite dashing in a shirt, blue blazer and matching chino's, and had was also wearing rather nice aftershave.

"Hello," she said happily, and stepped inside. He closed the door behind her and she turned to face him.

"Welcome home," he said, smiling.

"Home?" she said sweetly.

"When you are here, it's your home," he said.

She smiled and leaned forward, pressing her head against his chest. He awkwardly put an arm around her in a gentle hug. She sensed his unease and stepped back.

"So," she said, "do you want to show me my room?"

He smiled and held out an arm gesturing to the stairs so she led the way, taking directions from him when she reached the first floor. Eventually they arrived at a closed door at the foot of the stairs up to his master suite.

"I've put everything in here that's been delivered. If you want to get anything to make it feel homely just order anything you want," he said proudly.

Mary pushed open the door and was met with a large four poster bed, covered in pillows, cushions and perfectly laid white sheets. She didn't remember looking in here on Wednesday, so was genuinely pleasantly surprised when she saw it.

Around the room was a dressing table, two huge wardrobes, a sofa, a desk and chair, and another door.

"That's your bathroom," Edward said. "It's the only suite with a bath, so I thought you might like it."

Mary wandered in, it was larger than her whole room at university, and had a huge roll top bath, a separate shower, and a massive mirror.

"It's lovely," she said, unable to find any better words.

"Your deliveries are in the bottom of the wardrobes," he said. "Do you have a shopping list for me?"

"Oh, sorry," she said, rummaging in her handbag. She pulled out a slip of paper and passed it too him. "I could have bought mine over."

"No, this is your little palace, everything should be here for you," he said without thinking.

"Does that make me a princess?" Mary said childishly, beaming up at him sweetly.

"Yes, it does," he said smiling, relishing in her role play and clearly delighted that she was on board with it.

"Now, you get yourself all set up, have roam around the place, nowhere is off limits. I have to go and get your shopping list, and I'm going to get something really nice for us to have for dinner tonight. I'll be a few hours I imagine. If that's ok?"

"Of course," she said happily. "I'll be all unpacked and settled when you come home to me."

The 'to me' did the trick. He smiled and put a hand gently on her shoulder, then left the room and headed downstairs.

Mary opened the wardrobe and started pulling out parcel after parcel, arranging them on the floor. She'd finally pulled the last one out when she heard the door close, and Edward's BMW slid down the driveway as she watched from the window.

She was like a child in a sweet shop. There were hundreds and hundreds of pounds of clothes on the floor in front of her, and a whole mansion to go out and explore. She told herself to open the parcels and arrange her room first, then she would allow herself to go outside and have a cigarette, then explore the house.

It took her a while, but in just under an hour she had sorted her room, unpacked, and hung all of her clothes, and set up her dressing table. She made one big bag of recycling from the boxes and bags and headed off with her cigarettes to find the bins, and a quiet corner.

She'd realised early on that her 'act' wouldn't allow for smoking, so she felt like a teenager again, looking for a spot she could smoke while Edward wasn't around. It didn't take her long to find the bin store at the side of the house, which also seemed the perfect little smoking spot. She dumped the rubbish, smoked a couple of cigarettes back-to-back, then headed upstairs.

She had already decided to change her outfit for when he returned, so took off her clothes and sprayed a little deodorant on them to get rid of any trace of smoke, before dropping them into her laundry basket, along with her underwear, and put her shoes in the bottom of her wardrobe. She stood in her room, completely naked with her hands on her hips, spoilt for choice for what to wear.

She eventually settled on a short white tennis skirt, and a white t shirt. She pulled a white plain cotton bra and cotton pants from the drawer and decided to go barefoot for now. She put the outfit on and looked at herself in the mirror. Something was off. She realised that painted fingernails and toenails weren't in keeping with her character. She headed into the bathroom and quickly removed the paint from her nails, then let her hair down and brushed it straight down her back.

She returned to the mirror. This was the look she wanted for today. She checked her phone, then tucked it into her waistband as she went to explore the house alone.

She wandered from room to room on the first floor, but found only bedrooms, mostly smaller than hers, so sauntered up to his suite on the top floor. A quick inspection of his huge bathroom didn't turn up anything interesting beyond an assortment of nice smelling and expensive aftershaves. His dressing room was perfectly arranged and full of smart clothing, shoes, and accessories. His bed was huge, low, and if it hadn't been perfectly made, she would have rolled around on it. Given that she'd put on her new clothes and done her hair, and her lack of confidence in being able to put it back as she found it, she resisted.

She had a root around briefly in his bedside table, half expecting to find Viagra or condoms after a conversation she'd had with Louise, but there were none. It was quite disappointing in some ways, it seemed to Mary that he was exactly as wholesome as he made out.

She made her way downstairs and had a good look around, discovering a snooker room she'd missed the other day, and trying out each sofa she found, until she eventually went into his office, which was also a library. She casually flicked the mouse, and his computer woke up.

'*No password,*' she thought to herself.

The browser was open, and much as she didn't want to invade his privacy too much, the lure of his browsing history was too tempting. It seemed a first glance that he spent much of his computer time, of which there wasn't a lot, sorting banking and dealing with accountants, but he did seem to like to watch porn occasionally. She scanned the titles of some of the films he'd watched. Most of it was older men with younger women, some bondage and BDSM, and the remainder was threesomes and gangbangs. She wanted to watch a few herself but didn't have the time right now. She closed the browser and headed out towards the pool.

She walked through the door and dipped a toe in the water, it was warm. She went and had a look at the gyn, then the jacuzzi, and finally the steam room, then wandered outside down through the huge lawns under the trees. The autumn breeze caught her as she passed through the trees and found a tennis court and a secret little patio area at the back, with a barbecue and a summer house – a huge summer house. The cold biting at her arms and legs, she quickly made her way back to the kitchen. She'd just put the kettle on and made herself a coffee when Edward arrived home.

She heard him close the door, then a moment later he entered through the kitchen door.

"Hey there," Mary said sweetly.

"Hello, wow, you've got changed, you look pretty."

"Thank you," she said, putting down her coffee and giving him a twirl.

"All unpacked?"

"Yes, and I've put the rubbish in the in the recycling, and I've had a walk around the garden," she said proudly.

"Have you had any lunch?"

"No silly," she said, "I want to eat with you. I waited."

She turned her back to him and picked up her coffee, looking out across the lawn as she sipped it. She felt him come closer and stand behind her. She leaned back ever so slightly towards him. She waited for a hand to touch her, but it didn't. Instead, he stepped to her side and opened the fridge, pulling out a pre-prepared plate of sandwiches and a salad bowl.

"This ok for lunch?" he asked, "we're having lasagne later."

"Anything," she said, taking the seal off the sandwiches as he passed her a plate.

She took some sandwiches and some salad and went to sit at the table.

"Do we eat here, or in the dining room?" she asked.

"Here," he smiled. "The dining room is for entertaining. Maybe we'll do that sometime."

"That sounds nice," she said.

He made himself a plate of food and came and sat next to her at the table.

"Do you have any work to do today?" he asked as he started eating.

"No, not today, I'll do it tomorrow. Today I'm all yours," she said softly. He didn't look up, but Mary was sure the comment landed as she'd hoped. Getting a reaction was becoming a challenge she enjoyed.

"Anything you would like to do today?" he asked.

"Well, I was thinking after lunch I would love to go for a swim, then maybe have a bath and dress for dinner?"

He smiled. "I usually only swim in the mornings before breakfast," he said.

Mary had a feeling this was a test. A test she intended to pass. She looked up at him longingly and put a hand on his arm.

"But, pleeeeeease. Come swimming with me," she said.

She saw him melt, putty in her hands.

"Ok, just this once," he said, smiling back at her then returning to his lunch.

Mary was loving the interaction between them, and the more she looked at him, the more attracted to him she became.

"Thanks," she said, removing her hand from his arm slowly.

They ate in silence for a while, clearly enjoying each other's company with no awkwardness, then Mary took the plates to the dishwasher and walked back behind him, putting a hand on his shoulder. He instinctively lifted his hand to touch hers.

"I'd better go and put my costume on," she said. "Meet at the pool in five?"

"Ok," he said, clearly a little reluctant to let go of her hand.

She slid her hand off him and walked away from him quite slowly towards the door. She couldn't tell if he was watching her, but she was quite clearly letting him, if he wanted to.

Once through the door into the hall she raced upstairs and pulled out one of the new swimming costumes she had bought. It was reserved, classic, and white. She stripped and put it on, then pulled some white pumps from the wardrobe and tied her hair into a ponytail and putting on a short white cotton robe. Keen to be at the pool before Edward, she headed back downstairs after she heard him pass her bedroom door on the way up to his.

She went to the poolside and sat on a lounger, knees together, legs exposed, as he emerged at the poolside in a pair of tight trunks and a t shirt. He hesitated as he saw her sat there, then a sweet smile from Mary encouraged him to approach. Mary stood up and kicked off her pumps then undid her robe and let it fall to the lounger.

She saw the briefest reaction in his eyes.

"What do think?" she asked, spinning once in front of him.

"What?" he stuttered.

"Of my costume, silly."

"Oh, it's lovely," he said.

"Come on," she said encouragingly.

Edward took off his t shirt. Mary was impressed. She'd never seen a sixty-year-old man in tight trunks before, but in her mind they didn't look as good as Edward did. He clearly used his home gym a lot. She wanted to compliment him, but it would be out of character, so she didn't.

She held out her hand and he took it and led her to the pool. She walked down the steps as he watched her, then submerged her body into the water serenely, she then turned to face him.

"Come," she said.

He walked down the steps and slid into the water alongside her. They swam lengths together for a while, then he got out and sat on the side while Mary splashed around playfully for him. He eventually went and sat on a lounger, happy to just watch her swim around for as long as she wanted to. Eventually the novelty wore off a little, for today at least, and she decided to get out.

She swam to the shallows and stood, walking up the steps towards him. As she caught his gaze, she realised he was looking at her body. She looked down and realised that the white costume had turned almost transparent when wet, and she, and he, could see her breasts clearly though it, and a slight slit indented between her legs.

Mary feigned horror.

"I'm sorry, I'm so sorry, this is awful," she said, rushing to put on her robe. She sat next to him on another lounger and looked at him.

"I'm so embarrassed," she lied. It worked, it played to his role.

"It's ok princess. Luckily for you only I was here to see."

Marys inner submissive lit up and screamed at her in delight. She nearly smiled, but resisted.

"Thank you. Maybe I should go and bath and change for dinner?"

"Maybe you should," he said.

Mary walked away with a beaming smile on her face, unaware that Edward too smiled as she left.

A while later, Mary was relaxing in her massive bath when she heard something moving outside her bathroom door.

"Hello?" she called softly.

"Hi, it's just me, I bought up your hairdryer and straighteners, they're out here. Dinner will be in an hour."

"Thanks! You can come in and talk to me if you want to. I'm decent," she called back.

There was a brief pause, then the door handle turned and Edward slowly opened the door. Mary's body was covered in bubbles, with only her knees and her head and shoulders above water.

"See?" she said. "Come, sit for a while." She continued, nodding to the toilet.

Edward tested the integrity of the toilet lid, then sat down quietly.

"Five minutes," she said calmly.

"Sorry?"

"Five minutes to talk, then I'd sinking my head under the water and going back into character when I come back up, ok?"

"Ok," he said nervously.

"Tell me, what you're *really* looking for." Mary said encouragingly.

"My wife and I were sweethearts from school. She was my first, and only love. There has never been anyone else. She was bi, and we both developed a bit of a kink for younger innocent-looking women."

"I see. Hence, me?"

"We used to actively hunt them down, sometimes escorts, sometimes not, then invite them to the house and have them act as servants tending our every need. She wanted me to continue with it after she died. It's taken a few years to want to do it alone, but I wanted to get back into it so I started seeing girls from the agency in the hope one could act the part well enough for me to spend time some with her. Then eventually you came along."

"Did you have sex with them?"

"Yes, we both did. Sometimes together, sometimes not. I wasn't sure if this arrangement with you would go that way. It's been a while for me, and frankly you are the most beautiful girl I've ever seen, so I'm just happy to have you around to look at."

Mary paused and looked at her knees, responding carefully.

"I respond well to dominant older men. You are an attractive, dominant, much older man. I don't know why, but that makes this arrangement very easy for me, and I am more than happy to explore it, sexually or otherwise."

Edward looked down and smiled. She turned to look at him.

"But."

"But?" he asked.

"But, you cannot hold back. If you think something, say it. If you want something, tell me. Unless one of us says the word Unicorn which means we need to step back for a moment, I will never slip character again. Okay?"

He looked at her, swooning at her clarity and *dominance*, and nodded.

"What should I call you?" she asked.

"Sorry?"

"I have instinctively nearly called you daddy half a dozen times today, but that feels the wrong title to me. Do you have a preference?"

"Erm, no."

"Then inside this house I shall call you *sir*, unless we decide something else is more appropriate later, ok?

"Yes."

"Oh, and I think it would be beneficial if I stay overnight when I come."

Edward looked startled.

"In my room, on my own, at least to start with," Mary said, nodding at the door.

He looked relieved.

"It would do the arrangement good for me to stay for around 24 hours, don't you think?"

"Do you want more money?" he asked.

"I want nothing more than we have agreed already. And remember, you are paying for my time, anything else we do, is entirely consensual and is included in that time. Are we agreed?"

"We're agreed." Edward said, a little awkward at the conversation but seemingly grateful to have had it.

Mary smiled at him and sunk her head under the water, then popped back up and brushed the bubbles from her face.

She looked at him sweetly.

"I don't seem to be able to wash my back, would you mind?" she said, raising her voice back to it higher pitched sweetness. She sat up and leaned forward, keeping her chest in the bubbles, and passing him her sponge.

He stood up and sat on the edge of the bath and slowly cleaned across her shoulders and down her back silently. She sat there with her eyes closed as he slowly covering every inch of her back, then he put the sponge in the water next to her.

"There you go princess," he said. "Dinner will be in half an hour."

"Thank you, sir," she whispered as he stood up. She kept her head down as he left and closed the door.

Chapter 6

Mary climbed out of the bath shortly after Edward left, pleased with how the conversation went. She went into the bedroom to choose and outfit for the evening, and quickly settled on a knee length, short-sleeved white cotton dress and some new ballet pumps, again supported by a plain white bra and cotton panties. She dried her hair and straightened it, impressed with the rather expensive new hairdryer and straighteners she had chosen, then headed down to dinner. She bounced cheerily into the kitchen and stood beside Edward, who had just pulled his homemade Lasagne from the oven.

"That looks nice," she said. "And it smells even better."

"I don't get chance to cook it very often, when I have friends over there's usually too many of them for a homemade Lasagne."

"Friends come over?" Mary asked, curious to learn more about him.

"Oh, yes. Lots of friends, I might be a widower, but I'm not lonely," he said happily.

"Children?" Mary asked.

"A son, lives in Australia."

"Lovely," she replied.

By 'lovely' she meant she was relieved that a random family member probably wasn't going to turn up unannounced on a Saturday afternoon while a twenty-year-old "girl' was floating around his house in a short tennis skirt, but he missed that point, she thought.

"Pretty dress," he said, looking at her properly for the first time since she arrived in the room.

"Thanks!" she said sweetly, giving him a twirl.

They sat at the kitchen table for dinner.

"Would you like some wine?" Edward asked, picking up an open bottle of white.

"Ooh, yes please!" she said eagerly.

"Only a little for you though, I don't want you drunk."

'*Oh, you do...*' she thought to herself.

"Ok," she said.

Throughout dinner, Mary had to really concentrate on eating her Lasagne to avoid getting it on her new white dress.

"What are we doing after dinner?" she asked.

"I was thinking we could watch a film, if you like?"

"Whatever you want," she replied, smiling up at him.

"What kind of films do you like?"

"I like the films you like," she said, playing her role perfectly.

"Good, then I'll choose."

About an hour later they had cleared up and, being mid-October, the darkness had started to fall in. Edward loaded the dishwasher while Mary took their wine glasses and a bowl of peanuts into the conservatory, where Edward had said they would watch the film, and stood patiently waiting for him. He wandered in from the kitchen and put on some dim wall lights, then picked up a remote and a large screen came down from the ceiling and settled against the wall.

"Ooh, that's swish," Mary said, genuinely impressed.

He sat down on the sofa and selected a film. Mary knew straight away that he was trying to cater for her a little, despite not saying as much, as his choice of film wasn't something she would expect a sixty-year-old man to choose. In any case, she hadn't seen it, so that was a plus.

He sat down on the sofa, and she sat next to him, kicked off her shoes and bent her knees towards him, lifting her feet onto the sofa. She sat there for about twenty minutes of the film while she finished her second glass of wine, then became distracted from the film, and her inner submissive became playful. Mary tried to ignore the urge, but not for long.

She shuffled towards him and put her head on his shoulder, nuzzling into him a little. He didn't respond. She shuffled her head down onto his lap, and lay on her side, extending her legs out across the sofa, then decided to stay there a while.

After a few moments, she felt him move his hand, then start stroking her hair while she watched the TV. It was her turn not to react. She lay there for another ten minutes or so, enjoying his gentle attention, then rolled onto her back on the sofa, maintaining her focus on the tv, and lifted one knee, the dress rising a little as a result. She felt movement above her. She didn't look up, but she was sure he'd turned his head to look at her legs, which was entirely the point. For the next half hour, they stayed like that, but he stopped stroking her hair and simply rested one hand on her shoulder.

When the film finished, he flicked off the tv and she sat up. He looked at his watch.

"Maybe we should call your taxi," he said. "It's nine-forty-five."

"A taxi to bed?" she said sweetly. "It's a big house, but I can walk that far."

"You're staying tonight?"

"We said."

"Yes, but don't you need something to sleep in?"

"No, I have new nighties here. I bought some just in case," she said, smiling at him.

The look on his face was one of pure delight, though he tried to hide it.

"Maybe you should go and get ready for bed," he said.

"Will you come and say goodnight?" she asked.

"Yes, of course, I'll be up shortly."

Mary blinked at him and stood up, wandering slowly through the conservatory, kitchen and out into the hallway, then trotting more quickly to her bedroom.

She took off her dress and pulled a short pink nightdress from her drawers and put it on. It was very short, too short possibly, but she might get away with it, she thought.

She put it on, brushed her hair and her teeth and quickly checked her phone. There were messages from Louise. She didn't have time to answer them now, but she was going to be put to bed at ten, so she could answer Louise after Edward had said goodnight. She put the phone on silent, charging next to her bed and slid under the sheets. The bed was pure bliss, much better than the bed she had at university. She lay on her side and waited. A few moments later, she heard him coming up the stairs, then a knock at her door.

"I'm decent," Mary said, the irony of the statement amusing her.

Edward pushed open the door and smiled as he saw her wrapped up in her bed, He came over and sat on the edge of it, leaning back against one of the posters, making the frame creak a little.

"Comfy?" he asked.

"Amazing," she said happily.

"Then I should say goodnight and let you get to sleep."

Mary blinked.

"Oh, one second, I need to go to the bathroom, would you mind waiting?"

"Of course," he replied.

Mary, having intended this from the start, slid out from under the bed and walked across the room in her skimpy pink nightdress. She didn't look back, and simply made it look normal, comfortable, for him to see her like this.

Luckily, when she walked into the bathroom, she remembered she hadn't taken her pill, so fished the pack out of the small cosmetic bag she always carried with her and took it. She usually took it later as part of her normal bedtime routine, but tonight wasn't exactly normal.

She flushed the toilet and headed back into her bedroom. Edward lifted the sheets for her to slide in, then pulled them back down neatly over her.

"Goodnight then, princess," he said.

He turned and went to walk away.

"Wait!" she said.

He turned back and she pointed at her forehead. He smiled, and leaned down and kissed it. She murmured her approval.

"Goodnight, sir," she whispered.

He walked out and closed the door behind him.

Mary sighed and looked up at the ceiling, then climbed out of bed and wandered over to the door, locking it, and wandered over to the window. She opened it, to find a large flat roof behind it, which she assumed was part of the pool complex. She took off her nightie, tied up her hair, picked up her phone, and put on her outdoor coat before climbing barefoot out of the window onto the roof, pushing the window closed as much as she dared.

She fished her cigarettes out of her pocket and lit one, taking a long pleasurable drag on it in the cold night air. It had been a while. For as long as this 'arrangement' lasted with Edward, she was going to have to get used to it.

She opened her phone and read the messages from Louise.

'Hi, seduced the sexy old millionaire yet? X'

Then one an hour later, about twenty minutes ago.

'Hey, are you ignoring me or are you too busy fucking grandad? X'

Mary smiled and replied.

'Hi, no fucking. Cooks a mean Lasagne though x'

Louise, clearly at home, replied quickly.

'So, what are you doing now? x'

'He put me to bed at ten. Climbed out on roof to smoke and talk to you. x'

'You're on a roof? x'

'Flat roof, outside my bedroom window. In my knickers and a coat. x'

'Your bedroom? What the fuck? x'

'Come to mine tomorrow afternoon, pizza, and film night. Stay over, I'll tell you everything. x'

'You have yourself a date. x'

Mary put her phone back in her pocket and carefully put out her cigarette, discarding it into the guttering before climbing back through the window. She closed it, took off her coat, sprayed it in perfume a little and hung it in the wardrobe. She brushed her teeth again and rinsed with mouthwash just in case, then washed her face and sprayed on some of her new body mist Edward's credit card had bought for her. Then she slipped ack into her nightie and got back into bed. She lay there for a while, enjoying the comfort of the bed, then found herself drifting off to sleep.

She didn't know what time it was, but Mary was awoken in the night by a creak. She lay still, listening for anything else, but her room stayed silent. She opened her eyes slowly, sleepily, and realised there was more light in the room than when she went to sleep. Not a lot, but there was light from somewhere casting shadows in her room. She scanned the room with her eyes, keeping her head still, and realised her bedroom door was slightly open, and the light coming in was from the somewhere on the landing. She focused and could just see Edward standing in the doorway. She moved her head, very slowly, to get a better look.

He was stood still, looking at her in bed, wearing only a pair of cotton pyjama trousers. He had his hand inside them and was clearly playing with himself. Mary's mind was going to go one way or the other. It went *the other*. She lay there silently watching him, enjoying watching a guy masturbate for her, *about* her. She now knew for sure that she had an effect on him, regardless of how he tried to hide it. She found it kinky, and very arousing. He leaned a shoulder against the door frame as he continued. Mary moved her head again slightly, this time the light from the landing catching her in the eyes. Edward realised she was awake, and froze on the spot for a moment, then turned and disappeared from her door light a startled cat.

Mary felt guilty. If she'd stayed still this wouldn't have happened. She lay there for a few moments, deciding on her next course of action.

She decided she couldn't let this fester till morning, so she slipped out of bed and went across the landing and up the staircase to his room.

When she walked in the room was dark, aside from the shadows the moon cast through a skylight. Edward was lying on his side, almost foetal, with his back to her. She walked across the room silently and stood next to his bed, his thick carpet and her bare feet masking her footsteps.

"Sir," she whispered.

He heard her but didn't move, so she lifted the sheets and slowly climbed into his bed behind him. She shuffled over to him and lay on her side behind him, spooning him and putting her hand on his shoulder. He still didn't move. She desperately wanted to relieve his shame, he didn't deserve this, it was her fault, she thought.

"I had a lovely dream, but it woke me," she whispered, reaching her hand from his shoulder, tracing his arm until she found his hand and took it. He moved slightly to accept her grasp.

Mary had an idea.

"Was it a dream?' she whispered, letting go of his hand and placing hers on his chest, slowly sliding it downward until she felt the semi-rigid bulge in his pyjamas. She stroked his cock gently, it twitched. He straightened his legs a little. Her idea was working.

"No, it seems it wasn't a dream after all," she whispered, continuing to stroke him as his cock grew.

"Can I?" she asked sweetly.

He turned his head and looked at her for the first time, clearly torn between embarrassment and arousal.

"Please?" she asked again.

He rolled onto his back. She took that as a yes. She slid her hand gently under his pyjamas and took his cock in her hand. It was rock hard, and very well proportioned. Mary was impressed. He sighed, clearly enjoying himself. Mary got up on her knees and leaned over him, gently tugging the waistband on his pyjama bottoms, he lifted his pelvis slightly, allowing her to pull them down and release his manhood. She knelt next to him and looked into his eyes as she took hold of him once more, starting to work him slowly.

She saw his eyes sparkling, his stare fixed deep into her eyes in the shadowy silhouette she cast, sitting on his bed. She smiled at him, then slowly lay down, placing her head on his chest, looking down at his cock as she worked its length with her small dainty hand. She was playing the submissive, but right now she was completely in control. She had him in the palm of her hand, both literally and figuratively. She liked that, *a lot*.

She continued to work her magic on him for a while, enjoying laying on his chest and hearing his breathing changing as she slid her hand up and down his shaft. She was lost in the moment herself and could feel his climax building. She was tempted, sorely tempted to take him into her mouth, but resisted, as she wanted to finish him like this, to see him finish right in front of her eyes. After a few more moments, he started to grunt a little.

"You need to stop," he whispered.

"Do I?" she asked.

"No, yes, no, yes!" he replied, breathlessly.

"Why? Do you not like it?"

"Yes, but."

"But?"

"But I'm going to..."

"I want you to. For me," she said, smiling to herself. "It would make me happy to make you happy."

He groaned.

"Too late now," he said softly. Mary sped up her hand, then felt him tense. She slowed again as his juices started to flow, streams of cum flowing from his cock onto his abdomen in front of her eyes, some of it splashed onto Mary's cheek, but she was enjoying the sight in front of her so much she didn't care. Eventually, having covered himself in much more cum than Mary had seen from any of her lovers before, the flow from his cock stopped, and Mary gently let go of it.

She looked up and him and smiled as he tried to catch his breath.

"Look at the mess I have made," she said sweetly. She sat up and reached across for the box of tissues she spied on his bedside table. She wondered for a second if this was what the tissues were generally for. She sat next to him silently as she slowly and carefully used the tissues to mop up all his semen, smiling and being attentive throughout. When she was finished, the sat back on her heels and smiled at him.

"Unicorn," he said.

"What?"

"Unicorn, two minutes."

"Okay." She said.

"Is this..."

"Okay?" she asked.

"Yes."

"Edward," she started in her normal voice, "I came up here and started this. I flirted with you all day. I signed up to this. Unless I tell you something isn't ok, then just go with it and stop worrying, ok? It's fun, and as long as we're both having fun, I'm into it."

"If you're sure."

"I'm sure."

"It's been years Mary. I'm a little rusty."

"Seem fine to me," she said.

"Okay, if you're sure."

"I'm sure," she replied. "Unicorn."

Her expression changed to a beaming smile.

"Did I make you happy?" she said.

"Yes," he replied.

She bounced on her heels childishly.

"Can I make you happy again?"

"Maybe tomorrow, we need to sleep."

"Can I sleep with you?" she asked.

"Well, you are here now, why not," he said, clearly happy at the offer.

She lay down next to him as he pulled up his pyjamas, then lay facing him and put her leg across him. He wasted no time in putting his hand on her outer thigh and stroking her leg.

'He's getting there,' she thought as she drifted off to sleep.

Chapter 7

The next morning Mary woke alone in Edwards bed. She rolled around for a few moments, then got up to go and find him. She walked through the kitchen to find he'd laid the table for breakfast, there was a pot of coffee ready to drink, and some pastries on a plate on the kitchen island. Then she headed out to the pool.

"Morning sleepy," he said as she wandered onto the poolside, still in her nightdress.

"Morning, she said cheerily, sitting on a lounger as he swam over to her.

"Swim? It wakes you up."

"I only have the white costume so far, it wasn't appropriate, was it?" she replied.

"Oh, I could get used to it," he said, smiling, a little different in his approach to her this morning.

She smiled back.

"It's transparent, hardly worth going upstairs to fetch it really, is it?" she teased.

"No," he said calmly. "Swim?"

It took her a second, but she got it. She excitedly stood up at the edge of the pool, right in front of him. She very slowly lifted her nightdress over her head, exposing her breasts to him for the first time as she stood in front of him wearing only her white cotton panties. His eyes studied her body. She slid her hands across her hips to the waistband of her underwear, then slowly slid them off and stood in front of him naked.

"You like?" she asked, bending a knee slightly.

"I like," he replied.

She walked around the edge of the pool as he watched her, then slowly stepped in, and slid her body into the water, swimming over to him and resting her arms on the poolside next to him.

"How are you this morning?" she asked.

"Inspired," he replied, raising an eyebrow.

"Oh, really? How?"

"After breakfast," he said confidently, pushing away from the side of the pool and swimming away. Mary, curious, swam after him and they swam some laps together before he left her in the pool to go and prepare breakfast. About ten minutes later, Mary climbed out of the pool and put on a robe Edward had left for her and strolled into the kitchen.

She sat at the table and crossed her legs, rubbing her hair with a towel as Edward bought over a cooked breakfast and the plate of pastries. While they ate, she absently brushed her foot against his leg, which he allowed. When they had finished, Mary's curiosity got the better of her.

"What did you want to do now then?"

"Go and shower, then come to my bedroom," he said, a little hesitantly. Mary smiled, giving him his confidence back.

"Oh, really? what should I wear?"

"Something sweet."

Mary smiled and got up.

"I'll need half an hour to get ready for you."

"I'll be waiting."

Mary showered and picked out a short gypsy skirt and white cotton t shirt, then got ready quickly, eager to find out what Edward had in store for her. She made her way up to his room and knocked the door.

"Come in princess." He called.

Mary realised they were getting into character. She opened the door then put her hands behind her back, strolling sweetly towards him where he stood in the middle of the room wearing a dressing gown. The blinds were all open and the room was bathed in Autumn sun.

"I'm here as ordered," she said, standing in front of him. "What can I do for you?"

"Do you enjoy making me happy?"

Mary smiled.

"Oh, yes, very much."

"I'd like to explore that a little. What are you prepared to do to make me happy?"

"Anything."

"Anything?"

"Anything."

He paused and looked at her. She blinked and nodded, dropping character for a second to give him confidence to continue.

"Then when we have finished here, I will buy you some other clothes."

"Other clothes?"

"We'll talk about that next week."

"Okay," she said.

"For now, I'd like to know what you have learned."

"Learned?"

"To make me happy."

Mary hit character perfectly and stepped forward towards him.

"Now?" she asked sweetly.

"Please."

Mary bit her lip and looked up at him.

She reached forward and tugged at the belt on his robe. It fell open to reveal his naked body underneath. She stepped into his body and slid her hand down his abdomen and took hold of his soft cock, then looked up at him as she started to massage it. He looked down and smiled at her, tugging gently at the tie on the front of her skirt.

She stepped back and took off her t shirt, exposing her braless chest underneath, then tugged at her waistband and the skirt fell to the floor, leaving her naked in front of him. He raised an eyebrow.

"When you call me to your bedroom, I need to be prepared," she said.

She walked behind him and reached up to his shoulders, pulling back his robe and letting it fall to the floor before returning to stand in front of him studying his large manhood. She smiled to herself, then knelt in front of him, holding his cock against her cheek as she looked up. He was watching he, his eyes glistening. She maintained eye contact with him as she lifted it and slid it into her mouth. It took her a few minutes, which she put down to his age, but thanks to her attention his cock slowly started to lift and swell as she sucked on it. When it was stood to attention, Mary was becoming turned on herself. She stopped and looked up at him.

"You like?" she asked.

"I like," he replied.

"More?"

"Yes."

"You drive." She said, taking his hands and putting them on the side of her head.

She clearly woke something in him, as he wasted no time guiding her mouth back onto his cock and driving in deeper than she had taken him so far. He pulled her head back off him.

"Ok?" he asked.

Mary needed to deal with his nervousness once and for all.

"Let me show you," she whispered.

She stood up and bent over, allowing her to straighten her throat, then opened her mouth and slowly slid his entire length into her, adjusting her gag reflex a little to accommodate him.

"Oh princess," he moaned. "You are a good girl."

Mary slid off him and licked her lips.

"More?" she asked again.

"Yes."

She lay on her back on his bed, her head tilted off the end.

"I'm ready for you," she said softly.

He walked over quickly and slid himself into her mouth as he pinned her arms to the bed, then drove his cock into her throat. He held it there, watching her thrash around on the bed for air briefly, then withdrew and held it an inch from her face. Mary was in ecstasy at being in this position again, finally.

"Don't stop," she whispered.

He drove in again, and again, then eventually settled on a rhythm, enough to starve her of air just briefly while fucking her mouth quite forcefully. He continued for a while, much longer than Richard ever had, his age providing him with staying power. Mary couldn't quite believe she was being paid for this, one of her favourite activities.

They hadn't discussed her boundaries for sex. They hadn't planned to be in this position so why would they? But Mary got a little lost in her 'client', and decided they could have the conversation later.

Eventually, after much enjoyment for both, Edward withdrew. Mary whined in protest.

"I have to or I'll," he started.

"Would it make you happy?"

"It would make me very happy."

"Do it, do it please. I want to make you happy," Mary begged using her sweet voice.

Of course, it worked. He pushed back down on her wrists and drove into her, fucking her mouth with a sense of aggression Mary loved. She waited, and waited, then he roared as he slammed his pelvis against her face and drained himself into her throat. He came for an age, again. Mary was without air for much longer than she had ever been before, but he just kept coming, and right now she was prepared to pass out to drain him if necessary. Luckily, she didn't need to, and his orgasm subsided at the perfect time, him withdrawing as the last few drops of cum dripped from his cock into her open mouth. She swallowed the little in her mouth that hadn't made the direct path to her tummy, then moaned approvingly.

Edward sat down on the bed next to her, out of breath.

"Holy shit," he said.

"Did I please you?" Mary asked, wiping her face.

"Yes, well done princess," he said, kissing her on the forehead.

"Thank you," she said, her character and her real self both very pleased with themselves.

"I have to go soon, I should go and put some clothes on," she said. "Shall we pick this conversation up next week?"

"Oh, we definitely will," he replied.

Mary stood up and collected her clothes, giving him a cheeky smile before wandering naked back down to her room, tidying it, dressing, and making her bed, then making her way down to the hallway.

Edward came out of the kitchen, dressed.

"Unicorn," he said.

"This is getting to be a habit with you, isn't it?" Mary said, adopting her normal voice.

"I like it," he said, it's like an honesty card. "So, will I see you next week? Not scared you off? That was a bit intense."

"You *will* see me next week, you *haven't* scared me off, and that was just the right amount of intense. You've clearly watched more porn that I thought you had," she said, smiling.

"I've been living alone for five years, got to have a hobby!" he said, laughing.

"Good, watch some more, get more ideas, I like your style," she replied. "What's the deal with you shopping for other clothes?"

"Nothing you could wear in public, just around the house." he said, a little nervously.

"I like! Removing the innocence, a little I assume?" she asked.

"I like the servant in you. The submissive. I don't think I need you to act too innocent, I just like you to want to please."

"I love it! But you bought all those clothes? It's a waste."

"Next weekend, take what you want to keep, then we'll donate the rest. From now on, you'll wear what I choose."

"Unicorn," Mary said. She fluttered her eyelids at him. "Yes, sir."

He opened the door, and she stepped out of the house and into the waiting taxi, casting him a sultry glance as she closed the door.

About a mile up the street, her phone pinged. She had a notification from the bank that a thousand pounds had been paid into her account.

She looked out of the window and smiled to herself, then texted Louise.

'Hi, it got spicy. I'm also rich! Pizza and wine are on me. 2pm?'

'Slut! I need details! See you at 2. Xx'

Mary got out of the taxi at the university car park and immediately lit a cigarette, her first of the day. She made herself dizzy with the nicotine rush as she smoked it quickly and lit another, wandering slowly to her room, happy with how her weekend was panning out.

When she arrived back at her room, she tidied a little, made some lunch, then popped to the supermarket on campus for some wine. She was supposed to be working this afternoon, but the deadline wasn't tight, it could wait, and she was really looking forward to seeing Louise. She had a shower and popped on a pair of leggings and a t shirt, then sat on her bed, looking at holidays on her laptop. Her phone pinged. Edward had sent her a text.

'Hello, sorry I know my time is up for this week. Just need to ask for your sizes please?'

Mary typed a list and sent it to him.

'Thanks. I'll text you Friday to make sure everything is ok. Ok?'

'Yes, sir,' she typed. Pleased with herself.

She went back to her laptop and carried on looking at holidays until Louise arrived and knocked on the door. Mary opened it and Louise stepped in, instinctively kissing her hello. Mary's heart fluttered.

They lay on the bed together as Mary recalled the last 24 hours of her life to Louise, who was clearly impressed, and found the whole thing very sexy. Having had a date with Edward herself, Louise understood his charm, but didn't really share Mary's kink for men quite his age.

Eventually the conversation moved to booking a holiday, and Mary had a list of idea on her laptop which she shared with Louise. They looked through each of Mary's ideas, then Louise offered hers, she had just one.

"Where's this?" Mary asked, looking at the most stunning photos.

"On an island, near Jamaica."

"Jamaica?"

"Yeah, good right, our first holiday together should be a good one, we're earning it."

"I've seen enough, I'm in," Mary said, excitedly.

"Not yet sweetie. There's more," Louise said.

"More what?"

"It's adults only."

"No kids you mean?"

"No, that's not entirely what I mean, but there won't be any kids."

Mary looked confused.

"It's a swinger's resort for couples. Or at least, something like that. Could be a lot of fun."

"So, we go as a couple?" Mary asked curiously.

"Yes."

Mary looked at Louise, heart fluttering again.

"I'd like that," she said softly.

"Me too," Louise replied, putting a hand on Mary's knee.

"Are we a couple?" Mary asked, throwing her confidence on the floor for Louise to stamp on.

Louise closed the laptop and put it on the floor, then turned to Mary. They sat opposite each other with their legs crossed.

"Would you like to be a couple?" Louise said, taking Mary's hand gently.

"Yes, would you?" Mary said sheepishly.

"I'm already falling for you honey." Louise said, putting her arms around Mary. They hugged for a while happily, then Louise dropped a grenade into the conversation.

"We need to decide what we are doing about men though. I'm not giving up cock," she said, laughing hysterically.

"Me neither!" Mary agreed. "How about we separate it. Us, men, escorting, and just be honest with each other. It's not like we have anything to hide, is it?"

"See, that's why I'm falling for you." Louise said.

Mary leaned forward for a kiss. Louise put a hand behind her head and pulled her in for a deep, lingering romantic kiss. Mary swooned, feeling a depth of emotion she'd never felt before.

Louise sat back and looked into her eyes.

"We should eat pizza," she said. All this romance is making me hungry.

They made their dinner and booked a swanky suite at the adults-only hotel in Jamaica for two weeks next summer, confident their escorting would cover it in full in only a few weeks, then cuddled up on the bed together and put the TV on.

"Film?" Louise asked.

"Erm, we can do. Or..." Mary said.

"Oh, I get it. You didn't get any this weekend, did you?" Louise said smiling.

"No, neither did you." Mary said, "you refused him."

"If you had seen him, you would have too," Louise said, pulling a face. "We shouldn't have sex on our first date."

Mary looked disappointed. "We had sex before our first date," she protested.

Good point, Louise said, slowly climbing on top of her. "I take it I'm the boss, given your desperately slutty inner submissive?"

Mary's eyes sparkled as Louise took her wrists and pressed them either side of her head.

"Marry me?" Mary said, jokingly.

"Not yet," Louise said, smiling down at her. "But we're living together next year. Just the two of us, I want to wake up with you every morning."

She leaned down and kissed Mary's neck softly. Mary moaned. Louise smiled, then whispered in Mary's ear.

"Sorry baby, but we're not having hot sex on our first date."

Mary whined again.

"But I am going to make love to you all night."

Chapter 8

The next week was a little of a blur. Louise and Mary decided, initially, that they would keep their new relationship a secret for a while. At least that was the plan. Instead, they were inseparable, and held hands everywhere they went making eyes at each other. In the end, vodka caught them out at the student union on Monday night, when a little too much led to them making out quite publicly. Their secrecy lasted just a little over twenty-four hours. The reaction from their friends was beyond what they had expected. Some were a little surprised given their well-known liking for men, but all thought they made a lovely couple, and were happy for them. There were a few snide comments from a minority who really weren't really friends, but their sarcastic and homophobic comments were met with fierce resistance from those closest to them, including Elliot, who told Mary he had a feeling she would end up with Louise eventually.

Mary had accepted a booking from Monica for Wednesday night, as had Louise, who was going home this weekend so could only accept a weekday date. Mary was meeting Chris, a 40-year-old accountant, and Louise was meeting Alastair, one she'd met before and slept with a few times.

They got ready together at Mary's, both needing to be in the city for 7pm at restaurants not far apart. Louise and Mary had an open and honest conversation about their sex lives, and agreed that with their escorting work, they could sleep with any 'client' they wanted to, and that Mary should continue her fun and highly profitable arrangement with Edward, at least for the time being. They also agreed that sex with anyone other than an escorting customer required a conversation in advance, and that other women were entirely off limits.

They shared a taxi, arriving at Louise's restaurant first. Louise kissed Mary goodbye, then headed in as Mary arrived for dinner with the newest stranger, Chris. Dinner was nice, Chris was pleasant, and the sex was a little bland, but a satisfying midweek fuck. At two in the morning, tucked up in their own beds, they texted each other, discussing their customers for the evening, the sex they had both had, and then brushed it easily aside and moved on to their plans to move in together next year, their final year at university.

On Friday, Mary went over to Louise's to meet her parents, who were picking her up to take her home for the weekend. Louise introduced Mary to them as her girlfriend and Louise's mother was delighted, though her father seemed a little more reserved over the whole thing. When Mary got back to halls her mind turned to an impending overnight with Edward. Having not heard from him yet, she decided to contact him by text.

'Hi, eleven in the morning, ok?'

He replied quickly.

'Yes, see you then, looking forward to it.'

She allowed herself to get a little excited in the knowledge he was taking control of her wardrobe and had bought her some new clothes.

The next morning, she got up early and had a bath and dressed in tight jeans and an almost see through white top, then headed to his house for eleven. He welcomed her in and took her coat.

"Like my outfit?" she asked, in her "Edward' voice.

"I do, but. It's about to come off."

Mary smiled, "so soon?"

"Your clothes are on your bed. Go and change. I'll be in the kitchen." He turned abruptly and left. Mary, curious, headed upstairs. On her bed was a white PVC micro skirt, a white PVC bra, a white pair of fishnet hold-ups and some white patent high heels. She smiled. *'Kinky'* she thought to herself. She put the outfit on and looked at herself in the mirror, impressed with his choice, but not convinced white was the way to go. The skirt didn't cover her modesty hardly at all, and she decided it was no accident there was no underwear. *'If he makes me sit, he's going to enjoy the view,'* she thought.

She headed down the stairs and into the kitchen, where he was stood holding a coffee waiting for her. She walked seductively towards him.

"And this outfit?" she asked.

"Perfect. For daytime," he said, nodding to the stool in front of him.

Mary sauntered over to it and lifted herself onto it keeping her legs together a little and letting her feet swing. He stepped forward and put his hand on her leg as she looked up at him, already aroused at the chemistry in the room.

"Did you put underwear on?"

"No, sir."

"Let me check."

Mary opened her legs a little and he slid a hand up to her clit. She shivered pleasantly, then moaned, realising this was the first time he'd touched her there.

"Good girl," he said, removing his hand. "Drink?"

"Coffee please," she replied. He poured her a coffee and placed it on the marble kitchen worktop next to her, then stepped back.

"Thank you," she said.

"Don't drink it yet. It's too hot. I don't want you to burn your mouth, I'll need it fully functional later."

Mary was getting hornier and wetter by the second. This Edward was a good Edward. She smiled at him.

"Later?"

"Yes."

"So, what do I do while my coffee is cooling?" she asked.

He held out a hand and helped her off the stool, then nudged her legs apart with his foot. She helped. He grabbed hold of her hair and pulled her head back, so she was looking up at him.

"Does my servant kiss?"

"Yes, sir."

He leaned down and kissed her, forcing his tongue into her mouth roughly, Mary loved it. So much so that she didn't notice his other hand heading for her clit until it touched her. He stopped kissing her for a second.

"Open your legs wider," he commanded.

"Yes, sir." she said eagerly.

He quickly slid two fingers into her, the shock weakening her knees and she nearly fell.

"If you fall, this stops. Ok?"

She went to respond, but as she opened her mouth, he kissed her aggressively again and slid a third finger into her and started to finger fuck her quickly.

This was a predicament. Mary was horny, wet, and the speed his fingers were bringing her pleasure meant her knees just wanted to give up already. It was torture, blissful torture. Every time he thought she was going to orgasm, he stopped and made her stand there for a few moments, then started again. She wanted to hate it, but she really didn't. Eventually he decided she needed a little help, as he clearly wanted to deny her the orgasm, she desperately craved but keep her torture going. He let go of her hair and let her stand up, legs together for a moment.

"Coffee?" he asked.

"Thanks," she replied.

"Be quick, we're not finished."

Mary took a mouthful of coffee then put it down, he slid it away and pushed her forward, bending her over the cold marble worktop. For a moment she willed him to fuck her there and then. She should have known better. Instead, he bent down behind her and put three fingers back inside her, speeding up once more as he watched his work close-up. Mary screaming loudly, still wanted more.

She looked back over her shoulder towards him, he glanced up, looking for a reaction. She smiled at him and nodded before turning her face away and putting her cheek back on the marble worktop. He slowed his hand and she felt herself starting to be stretched as he slid in a fourth finger, she relaxed a moaned, the fullness of the feeling washing over her. Then she felt him push, gently at first, then more firmly. She quickly realised what he was trying to do, and held her breath, trying to relax as best she could. A moment later she felt the pressure release and her sex fill, gripping his wrist.

'Fuck, he's got his hand in me,' she thought.

He slowly withdrew it, making her scream as his knuckles passed her opening, and pushed it back in, doing it again and again until Mary could comfortably accept him. Mary liked trying new things, and this was new.

Andrew stood up and leaned over her.

"Can you squirt?" he whispered.

"Yes," she replied.

"Would you like to?" he asked.

"Yes please," she replied.

He put one hand on her back, and slid his hand back inside her opening, and upped the tempo.

Mary wailed in pleasure, losing control of herself. It was only moments later that she started to hear liquid, lots, and lots of liquid, flowing from her body, running down her legs and splashing outwards onto the floor as she had a massive orgasm. Edward clearly liked it, as he just continued doing it until she could squirt no more, and he quickly withdrew his hand, leaving Mary shaking and moaning uncontrollably on the worktop as he stepped back and watched, clearly pleased with himself for what he'd done to her.

Mary lay there for a few minutes as she calmed down, her body still twitching a little as she eventually stood and looked at him.

She smiled. He smiled back.

"I should go and clean up," she said.

"Yes, you should," he agreed. "Take a shower, I'll put a new outfit out for you on your bed after I have mopped this up."

"Yes, sir," she replied, gingerly walking away, her pelvis aching slightly – but in a good way.

She showered for a while, enjoying the hot water running down her body. When she walked back into her room, she was met by a black crotchless fishnet catsuit lying on the bed, with a pair of black boots. She put them on and looked in the mirror, keen to see how she looked having never worn anything like it before. She loved it, and quickly took a few seductive selfies in it to show Louise then went downstairs.

As she strolled into the kitchen, Edward had cleared the floor and had made lunch. He turned to look at her as her heels started clicking on the kitchen floor. Her crotch was completely exposed, as was her rear, but the rest of her body was covered in the fishnet material which didn't provide any privacy but made her feel sexy. She confidently strolled over to him and leaned against him.

"Good choice," she said, smiling.

"There's plenty more where that came from," he said. "Sit, you must be hungry."

As they sat, Mary wanted to talk.

"Unicorn," she said softly.

"Now you're at it!" he said.

"Sorry. Just..."

"I'm joking, go on," he said warmly.

"So, is this what you and your wife used to do? Bring sub girls over and use them sexually?"

"Mostly yes. You would be amazed how many girls were up for it. They would come over and dress how we wanted, then we'd all just have sex all weekend."

"I'd have liked your wife," Mary said absently. "My kind of woman."

"Yes, you would, and she would have *really* liked you. She had a thing for tiny, beautiful blondes."

"Did you do it a lot?"

"Yes, for years. Occasionally we'd have a male over, sometimes a few girls. Sometimes we'd have parties."

"Parties? What kind of parties?"

"Gangbangs mostly. Ellen, my wife, would get one or two of the young girls together and we would have a poker night for my friends. They were part of the entertainment."

"Your wife too?" Mary asked curiously.

"No, we would just direct the girls on what to do and with who."

Mary stirred her pasta around with her fork.

"Wow," she said. "How many friends?"

"Usually between four and six. Disgusted?" he asked.

"Quite the opposite," she said, smiling. "Sounds quite hot to be honest. When's your next poker night?" she laughed.

"You're joking, right?" he said hopefully.

"Yes, I am. I'm not sure my little body could take being used by a group of men all night, no matter how appealing it sounds. I would have to start with two and build my way up," she laughed. "Back to today?"

"Yes, today. I do have a question, while we're chatting."

"Oh, go on."

"How do you feel about photographs or video?"

"I'm fine with either, just don't show my face. I don't want a video of me having my face fucked landing on the internet in my thirties and ruining my career."

"Fine by me," he said. "And while we're on that subject."

"Unicorn!" They both said at the same time and laughed.

Mary looked down for a second to get back into character and then looked up.

"I've finished my dinner, did you want to use my mouth now?" she said. In character but meaning every word.

"Go to my room and wait for me," he said.

"Yes, sir," Mary replied, heading through the door, and trotting happily up the stairs.

• • • •

A bout an hour or so later, Mary was in the pool, in a less revealing costume than last week, while Edward sat admiring her with a coffee from the sun loungers. She was processing everything that had happened that morning, from a quite literal screaming orgasm bent over the kitchen counter to having spent the last hour having her mouth used for Edwards pleasure. Her inner submissive kept telling her that it was wrong to be paid for this, it was too much fun. However, her mind ran over her blossoming relationship with Louise, and how Louise was beginning to show the kind of dominance behind closed doors that she craved. She could walk away from this in a heartbeat, it was just fun, she couldn't walk away from Louise, she was so much more.

Mary also wondered if Edward was planning to have sex with her at any point. He hadn't suggested it yet but given how good he had been at other activities, Mary thought that sex with him would probably be quite fun.

She spent much of the afternoon swimming and relaxing by the pool while Edward went out shopping for dinner, then when he returned, she put on a robe and headed into the kitchen.

"Anything particular I should wear this evening after my bath, sir?" she asked.

"It will be on your bed ready for when you come out," he replied, kissing her on the forehead.

She smiled at him and went upstairs to get ready for the evening ahead.

When she had finished her bath, she curiously opened the bathroom door, having heard him go into her bedroom a little earlier. On her bed was a pair of black glossy stockings, a suspender belt, and a black leather collar with a metal loop on the front of it. On the floor stood a pair of knee-high black high-heeled boots. The absence of a thong or g string or any other panties was clearly no mistake. She put them on and took another selfie for Louise, straightened her hair, and headed downstairs for dinner.

As she entered the kitchen she saw a leather lead, with a metal clasp on it sat on the kitchen worktop. He turned and picked it up, beckoning her over.

"Dinner isn't ready for a while yet," he said, clipping it to her collar as she reached him. "Come with me."

Mary tingled all over. Just the presence of the collar was pushing all her buttons.

He led her, using the lead, through the cellar door and down to the garage, flicking the lights on as he went. When they arrived in the garage Mary was stunned. She hadn't been down here before, and had already seen the BMW and the Aston Martin, but there was also a Ferrari, and a Bentley.

"Pick one," he said.

"What?" she blurted out. "I mean, what sir?"

"Pick one, the one you like the most."

She pointed at the Ferrari.

He pulled the lead and led her over to it.

"I'll take you out in this tomorrow, if you are a good girl tonight, ok?"

'I'd have been a good girl without the car' she thought.

"Yes sir, ok sir," she said.

"Good. You look amazing by the way," he said, smiling.

"Thank you," she said, shrugging sweetly.

He led her back to the kitchen, removing the lead while they ate their dinner in a sexually charged silence.

When they had finished, she sat patiently while he cleared the plates, then he took her to the snooker room, again using the collar and lead.

"I want you to climb onto the table and pose for me," he said, picking up a camera from a table.

Mary didn't hesitate, using a chair to step up onto the snooker table and lying down. Over the next half an hour he took photos of her lying seductively, close ups of her legs and lingerie, shots from behind to cover her face, and then they moved onto close-ups of her clit, sex, and ass with her body in a variety of positions. Mary loved the whole experience, and so did he.

"I'll be sending some of these to my poker club, to give them a flavour of what they are missing, to show them my princesses assets," he said confidently.

Mary, confident her face wasn't in any of them, was really turned on at the thought of him sharing intimate photos of her with his friends.

"They will all want to fuck you."

"And if you could, would you let them?" she teased.

"That depends."

"On what?" she asked.

"I have a reputation to maintain. My parties are of a high standard. I would need to know you could satisfy my guests to those standards," he said dismissively.

"And how would you know that?"

"I would know because you are going to go to my room and wait on my bed for me while I lock the doors and turn the lights off, then you are going to show me."

'Finally,' Mary thought happily.

She climbed down from the snooker table and stood against him, looking up.

"Yes sir, I *really* am."

His eyes glistened as she turned away and pressed her ass against his groin and bent over, then stood up and headed to the foot of the stairs. She stood in her lingerie, one foot on the first step and the other on the second, holding the rail as he passed, admiring her body, then she wandered off to his room.

The room had already been set with dim light, and Mary sat on a chair to take off her boots, then her bra, leaving only her collar - lead still attached - and stockings and suspender belt. She wandered around the room, excited, and turned on with anticipation, until she heard him coming up the stairs. She quickly headed onto his bed and arranged herself seductively, on her side with one leg bent over the other facing the door.

He walked in and looked at the vision in front of him. He was clearly a little nervous, finally taking up the option to have sex with her, and Mary decided to help calm his nerves.

"Hello sir. I took off my boots and bra, I hope you don't mind."

"Not at all," he said, as Mary slid off the bed and wandered over to him silently in her stocking feet.

She reached up and unbuttoned his shirt slowly, staring into his eyes, then pushed it back for him to pull off properly. As he pulled of his shirt, she set to work on his belt, then trousers, then boxers. It didn't take Mary long at all to have him stood in front of her naked. She turned once more and pressed her ass against his groin and bent over, though this time he took her hips and pulled a little, his soft cock brushing against her sex.

She stood and turned to him.

"Need my mouth, sir?" she asked.

"No, you need mine," he said, taking the lead and pulling her aggressively over to the bed. "Lie down and open wide."

Mary giggled a little, scooted onto the bed quickly and rolled onto her back, pulling her legs up and apart. He was on her in a flash, his tongue probing her opening. Mary reeled in surprise at how fast he moved, and how keenly he went down on her. He worked her sex and clit, hands-free for nearly half an hour, slowing occasionally to delay her orgasm as she moaned endlessly. Eventually he sat up and Mary noticed that his cock was now rock hard and ready for action.

He climbed above her and slid a hand under the pillow next to her head, retrieving a condom, then sat between her legs opening the packet.

"Allow me," Mary said softly.

She sat up and took it from him, then leaned down and gently sucked his cock for a second before rolling the condom on slowly.

"There, looks like we're both ready," she said, laying back and staring at him invitingly. He leaned forward and Mary reached out, guiding his cock into her. Once his tip had breached her opening, he pressed his length firmly into her. She gasped loudly.

"Fuck me, please sir," she begged softly as she lifted her legs and wrapped them around his body. Edward didn't need telling twice. He slid back and impaled her body on his cock with a force she'd not experienced since Richard.

"More," she howled desperately.

He leaned back and grabbed her ankles, pressing them above her head, folding her body in half, and slammed into her again.

"Oh my fucking god, yes!" Mary screamed.

For the next ten minutes it became a game. The harder Edward fucked her, the harder she wanted him to. Mary was lost in him being a customer, right now he was giving her exactly what she had missed. When he pulled out, she nearly cried, but his instruction to roll over was carried out quickly and he pulled her up onto her knees in a flash and was inside her once more, grabbing hard onto her hips as he slid into her over and over.

"Ride me," he instructed, pulling out of her, and lying down. She quickly climbed onto him and guided his cock into her. He grabbed the lead and pulled as she ground her pelvis down onto him, thrusting her into the air as he arched his back, the two of them eventually coming loudly at the same time, Marys legs shaking violently as he filled the condom inside her. Once they'd both finished, he let go of her lead and Mary slowed to a gentle rhythmic gyration in her pelvis for a few moments before slowly climbing off him.

He stood to go to his bathroom, out of breath.

"Did I do well?" she asked, lying on her front with her legs bent into the air.

He stopped and looked at her, a smile right across his face.

"Perfect princess, perfect," he replied.

Chapter 9

Over the next month or so, Edward regularly took advantage of having a very willing Mary on tap every weekend. Louise really enjoyed hearing the stories, then *really* enjoyed the sex she and Mary would have afterwards, exploring Mary's submissive side herself.

In the run up to Christmas, Edward told Mary that he had decided to go and visit his son's family in Australia in the new year, so her visits to his house would end just before she went home for Christmas, at least for a few months. Mary was fine with it, having made an obscene amount of money from him and her other escorting work, and had enough saved to pay for her holiday with Louise next summer, spending money, and enough left to put the deposit down on the lovely three-bedroomed apartment she and Louise had viewed for next year.

Mid-December, with the holiday paid off and the apartment reserved, Mary headed over to Edwards house for one last time. When she arrived there was a rather expensive Mercedes sat on the drive, which she assumed was another of Edwards purchases. When he opened the door for her, she stood on tiptoes and gave him a kiss on the cheek, then turned to the car.

"This is nice. Treated yourself again?" she asked.

"No, I have a friend here for coffee, so, unicorn?"

"Oh, ok. Want me to keep out of the way?" she said.

"No, he's a poker club guy, knows the score, as it were. Come meet him?"

"Of course!" Mary said obligingly.

Edward led her into the kitchen, where his friend stood holding a coffee leaning against the kitchen worktop.

"Allan, this is Mary," Edward said, almost proudly.

"So it is," Allain said. "Pleased to meet you, Mary. So, you're the one who has been distracting him and stopping us booking a poker night?"

Mary smiled and shrugged.

"I can see why," Allan said, leaning down to give her a kiss on the cheek as she approached him.

She smiled again. Allan was clearly younger than Edward, in his early fifties, she thought.

"Coffee?" Edward asked her.

"Please," she replied, confidently slipping up onto a stool in front of them.

"You wear more than the others he's had here," Allan said, gesturing to her new, rather expensive leather trousers.

"Only when we have company," she said, smiling at him and winking as Edward passed her a coffee.

The silence she caused with the statement was deafening.

"Well, I need to get off and leave you two to your final evening together," Allan said, putting down his mug. "It was lovely to put a face to the photographs."

Mary smiled, remembering Edward had said he would send some to his friends.

"I hope it wasn't a disappointment?" she asked.

"Certainly not," he said, picking up his coat from the back of a chair and heading to the door with Edward following him.

"Lovely to meet you, Allan," Mary said as he left the room. She smiled to herself.

When Edward returned, he came and stood where Allan had been, right in front of her. She crossed her legs on the stool, pushing one foot into the air, which she used to stroke Edwards leg.

"Okay?" she asked.

"Yes, thanks for that. He made an excuse to meet you while he had the chance."

"I guessed."

"He *really* liked the look of you."

"I guessed that too."

"Shame it's our last night, I might have asked him to stay a while," Edward said, a little suggestively and testing the water.

"For what?" Mary asked, knowing exactly what he was suggesting.

"For you to entertain for me," he replied.

Mary took a sip from her mug. She thought about it for a second, then decided to give Edward a last night together to remember.

"What's he doing tonight?" she asked.

"I don't know, why?"

"Ask."

Edward picked up his phone and dialled Allan, who was driving home, and put him on speaker.

"Allan, Mary was wondering what you are doing tonight." Edward said.

There was a pause.

"Nothing, why?"

"Why don't you come back over after dinner? Around seven?" Mary said confidently.

"Really?" he asked.

"Really." Mary replied.

"I'll be there."

"Good, see you later!" Mary said brightly. Edward finished the call.

"Really?" he asked, his expression one of sheer excitement.

"Really!"

"Thank you, Mary," he said, clearly delighted.

"Unicorn," she whispered. "Swim?"

"Absolutely," Edward said. "Wear the white one."

Mary smiled and slipped off the stool to head to her room. "Yes, sir," she said as she walked away.

A few hours later, after having had an early dinner, Mary was relaxing in her customary Saturday evening bath. She heard Edward enter her bedroom and put out an outfit for her, as he did every Saturday evening while she was in the bathroom, then leave again. She was more than a little excited for what the evening might hold, and she called Louise to tell her what she was up to. Louise, having been in bed with two men on more than one occasion in the past, was very encouraging, and told Mary to make the absolute most of her last evening with Edward.

After she had finished her bath, she went into her bedroom to a black, skin-tight latex minidress, fishnet hold ups, black knee-high boots, and her collar. She put them all on, dried her hair, sent Louise a selfie, then sat on her bed listening for Allan to arrive.

At a few minutes to seven she heard the front doorbell, then Edward let Allan in. She gave them a few minutes to get a drink, then headed down the stairs into the snooker room, where they were sat where Edward told her they would be, drinking whisky.

Earlier in the day, Edward and Mary had discussed how this would all start, and she was keen to play the part perfectly, so she silently walked over and stood about a metre in front of them, her head owed a little, hair covering her face, waiting, listening.

"She looks better than her pictures. If that's possible." Allan said.

She smiled to herself beneath her hair.

"Take closer look if you want," Edward said.

Allan put his drink down and stood, walking over to Mary, and circling her slowly, closely. He stopped in front of her.

"Anything underneath?" he asked.

"No," Edward replied.

"Mind if I?"

"Of course not," Edward replied. "Open your legs princess."

Mary shuffled her right foot outward a little as Allan reached under her skirt and slid his fingers over her clit. She resisted reacting, though it was difficult.

"Feels as perfect as it looked in the photos." Allan said.

Mary smiled to herself again, becoming wetter by the second as the role play continued.

"Shall we take her upstairs?" Allan asked.

"Here," Edward said, passing him the lead to her collar, "she'll respond to you if you're holding this."

Allan took the lead and slowly reached under her chin and clipped it to her collar. As soon as the clip was closed, she looked up into his eyes and smiled.

"Hello, sir," she said sweetly.

"There's that beautiful face," Allan said. He tugged on the lead, pulling her towards him. She leaned against his body as he slid his free hand behind her and squeezed her behind.

Edward, clearly feeling a little left out, stood.

"Allan," he said, holding out his hand. Allan passed him the lead and he pulled her from Allan's grasp over to him. She stood against him in the same way.

"Something only for me," Edward said to Allan. "You can't do this."

He reached up and grabbed her hair and pulled, tilting her head back. Mary opened her mouth waiting for him to kiss her, she knew he would. He leaned down and kissed her aggressively as she stood against him, arms still by her sides.

"We're taking you upstairs Princess."

"Yes, sir," she panted.

They picked up their whisky glasses, Allan grabbed the bottle, and Edward led Mary by her lead, walking slightly behind them as they headed up to his room. When they arrived the two men chatted as Mary was left standing at the foot of the bed while they took off their clothes. They both walked over to her and stood facing each other either side of her.

"Be a good girl princess," Allan said, gesturing at his cock. She looked to Edward for permission, he nodded. She knelt and took Allan's cock in her mouth while Edward watched working it until hard, then turned her attention to Edward, doing the same to him.

"You're restrained tonight, princess," he said.

Mary smiled.

"Can I?" she asked eagerly.

"Yes," he replied.

She lay on the bed on her back, tilting her head off the bed.

"Watch this," Edward said to Allan, as he stepped over and slid his entire length into Mary's mouth with ease.

"Fucking hell," Allan replied.

"She loves it, she'll do it all night given the chance, won't you princess?"

Mary moaned a little, unable to speak with her mouth full.

"Want to try?" Edward said, sliding out of Mary's mouth, causing her to moan in disappointment.

"Yeah!" Allan said.

"Want to try a different one princess?" Edward said, looking down at Mary, clearly checking she was happy to. She smiled and reached out to Allan's cock, taking is in her hand and pulling him forward.

"If she pushed on your thighs, pull out, it means she needs a breather. Okay?" Edward said to Allan. Mary loved that he did that, despite the role play he was still looking after her.

"Okay," Allan replied, sliding slowly into Mary's throat.

He wasn't a big or long as Edward, so Mary had no difficulties accommodating him.

"Wow," Allan said, clearly not used to the sensation.

"Let me show you how it's done," Edward said.

Allan slid out and watched as Edward repeatedly thrust his cock into Mary's throat, holding there while she writhed a little before letting her breathe again.

"Like that, see?" Edward said.

They swapped places again, and Allan replicated Edwards actions perfectly, which Mary really enjoyed. After a while they both stopped, and went over to get a drink, as Mary stood up. Edward nodded to her, and she peeled off the dress, leaving only her boots and hold-ups. Edward picked up a condom and passed one to Allan.

"Anal?" Allan asked.

Mary, stood over the other side of the room and now as horny as she could ever remember, had to stop herself speaking. She really, *really,* wanted to shout yes across the room, but didn't.

"No," Edward said. "We've never done it, and this isn't the time to start."

Mary wanted to stamp her foot in frustration, but didn't, instinctively she knew that he was right. Edward slid on his condom, Allan didn't. Mary knew what that meant. She turned silently and crawled onto the bed on all fours as Edward took up position behind her and Allan in front. They both leaned in and entered her, Mary almost came there and then. The sensation of having a cock in her mouth and sex at the same time was incredible. She tried to focus on pleasuring Allan with her mouth while Edward pounded away at her from behind, but Edward had learned exactly how she liked sex, and was really pushing her buttons. Eventually Allan pulled out of her mouth and simply watched as Mary became louder and louder, screaming in ecstasy as Edward started to groan and filled the condom, making her come too. As Edward slowed his thrusts, she turned to Allan and mouthed 'condom' at him. He realised he wasn't dressed for what was next and headed to the packet he'd left by his drink, quickly slipping the rubber on. As Edward withdrew from Mary's body, she quickly rolled over, lay on her back, and opened her legs wide. Allan wasted no time in going over and sliding his cock into her opening.

"Fucking hell you feel good," he said.

"Thank you, sir," Mary whispered.

Edward came back from the bathroom and sat in a chair with his whisky, watching patiently while his friend fucked Mary. Allan wasn't as aggressive or fulfilling as Edward, but Mary was so horny having two guys' attention that it didn't matter. She rubbed her clit as he thrusted into her, timing her orgasm to match his, both coming loudly at the same time and Allan collapsing onto her body. After a short moment, he lifted his weight and withdrew from her body, kissing her on the forehead as he got up and headed to the bathroom himself.

She lay on her front on the bed, lifting her feet into the air and pointing her boots to the ceiling, smiling sweetly at Edward.

"Did I do okay, sir?" she asked.

"Perfect as ever princess," Edward replied.

When Allan returned from the bathroom, he started to dress. Edward looked over at Mary and mouthed *'Unicorn'* to her. She smiled.

"Are you leaving us, Allan?" she said.

"Yes, sorry, this is your last night, I should probably be getting off. Great acting by the way Mary, you will win an Oscar one day."

"My degree isn't going to be in acting, but thanks!" she said, smiling up at him from the bed.

When Allan was dressed, Edward put on a bathrobe to see him to the door, and Mary stood up and gave him a hug.

"Lovely to meet you," she said, heading back to Edwards bed and lying back down.

"You too, really, thank you. A memory I won't forget," he said, turning and leaving the room with Edward.

Mary unzipped her boots and took them off, then the collar and the fishnets. She rolled around naked on Edwards bed for a few moments happily, then he eventually returned carrying a tray with snacks, wine, and water on it.

"You undressed," he noted as he put down the tray.

"You bought snacks and wine!" Mary said, getting up and wandering over to stand next to him.

"That was fun," she said, "if not a little shorter than I anticipated."

"Yeah, he tends to do that, he's always been a come and go guy."

"Not a bad thing tonight," Mary said.

"Why is that?"

"I get you to myself one last time, silly," she said, nudging him with her shoulder.

"Now did you want Mary for once, or the princess?"

"Difficult choice," he said.

"I suggest Mary," she said, sliding a hand into his dressing gown and stroking his cock.

"Any why is that?" he asked, his cock twitching at her touch.

"Because Mary absolutely loves anal. And when she's had a glass of wine, she's going to demand you fuck her in the ass," she replied, leaning down and taking a glass of wine from the tray.

"If I'd known earlier..."

"You know now," she said softly.

"Mary it is."

"Thought so," she said seductively, then smiled happily to herself.

Epilogue

After leaving Edwards for the last time, she wondered if she would ever see him again. He was staying in Australia until at least Easter, and a lot can happen in that time, particularly in the life of a student. As she sat in the taxi, with 4 suitcases of sexy lingerie, and mostly latex and leather dresses, and everything else he had ever bought her on her way back to campus, her phone pinged with his deposit into her account. It was at that point she knew their arrangement had come to an end. Edward had transferred ten thousand pounds into her account with the reference *'thank you. xx'* instead of his usual one thousand and *'Edward'.* She looked out of the taxi window and smiled to herself, fondly remembering their Saturday evenings together.

When she arrived at campus Louise was patiently waiting for her to help with the suitcases. Mary told her how much money Edward had transferred, Louise coming to the same conclusion about their arrangement being permanently over.

"It's a good job our apartment has three bedrooms, with all your expensive sexy gear to hang up," Louise said, laughing.

"It's all ours to share," Mary replied. "I can't wait to model some of it for you and see you in some of it."

"Me neither," Louise said. "I was thinking, maybe we have one bedroom as our dressing room, and one as our bedroom."

"And the other?"

"I don't want men in our bed. It's our bed, just for me and you, we can use the other one for entertaining," Louise said thoughtfully.

"I like your thinking," Mary replied, trying to pull two suitcases and smoke at the same time.

"Anyway, for now we have a sexy holiday to look forward to," Louise said excitedly.

"Yes, we really do," Mary replied. "And I can't wait to see what we get up to there."

Don't miss out!

Visit the website below and you can sign up to receive emails whenever P.T. Brown publishes a new book. There's no charge and no obligation.

https://books2read.com/r/B-A-BVXX-JNYIC

BOOKS 2 READ

Connecting independent readers to independent writers.

Also by P.T. Brown

Mary's Erotic Adventures
Mary's Awakening
Mary's Evolution

Standalone
Sophie's Hotwife Adventures

Ingram Content Group UK Ltd.
Milton Keynes UK
UKHW010628140723
425136UK00001B/60